Shrouded Deception

Stella Mace

Copyright

Copyright © [Year of First Publication] by [Author or Pen Name]
All rights reserved.

Also by Stella Mace

Alex Harper Mystery Series
Shrouded Deception

Mia Conrad Mystery Series
Shattered Echoes

Parker Rose Mystery Series
Small Town Shadows
Small Town Secrets

Standalone
Silence of Secrets

Remembrance

Present day...

The sound of dirt hitting the wooden lid rouses me. My brain and body compete to figure out where I am, but there's only darkness. The voices gradually drift in as mounds of dirt hit the wood like a hailstorm. I start to panic, and I know from experience that panicking won't help. I slowly try to work out the dimensions of the box in my head.

A searing pain tears through my right side as I lift my hands to push against the top. I wince uncontrollably and touch my head with my left hand. I can feel the lukewarm, sticky liquid beginning to clot on the side of my head. I try to remember what happened and where I am, but nothing comes to me. The only thing I know is that I have to get out of here.

I hear the voices fade. The lid gives way a little. It's not a coffin but feels more like a box. I consider kicking against it but realize that the noise will attract too much attention. Whoever is doing this has no fear of time or being caught. Leaving in the middle of burying someone alive isn't smart, but they must think that I'm dead.

Dirt falls into the box as I push against it, and I need to control myself again as I taste blood. The dirt in my mouth causes panic to rise from the pit of my stomach. After a few shoves, I figure out that something is keeping the lid in place. A lock? I try to stay calm as I contemplate my next move.

Should I scream? Maybe there's some humanity left in whoever's doing this, and hearing that I'm still alive will make them rethink their plan. Unlikely. Anyone who can come this far is likely to want to cover their tracks, and if that means hastily shoveling the remaining sand on me, so be it. Think, Alex! Think! I trace my way down the opening to find the chain or bolt that's keeping me trapped in here. I find it and try to make out what it is through touch in the pitch dark.

"Come on...come on ...please!?"

I don't know why I'm whispering as if there's someone out there who's coming to save me, but it helps me. It makes me feel less alone and hopeless. The lock feels flimsy. This wasn't well thought out.

"Amateur hour." My cockiness gets dealt a swift blow by my brain. "We're not out of this yet. Maybe save the gloating for when you're free. And safe!"

It's tougher than I'd thought to break the flimsy chain keeping the lid shut. I don't have much time before their smoke break or whatever is over, but I can't give up. I push through the pain and lightheadedness to keep trying to break out.

Eventually, I hear the crack of the chain being released from the plywood. I stay still for a few minutes, unsure of whether they heard it too. When I don't hear movement or sound, I decide that it's safe for me to get out. The mounds of dirt on the lid are another obstacle, but thankfully, adrenaline and the survival imperative are a formidable combination. I creep out of the box and quietly replace the sand to give the impression that it's not been disturbed.

I crouch in the corner of the grave. It freaks me out that I'm standing in my own grave, but I quickly figure out that I wasn't the intended beneficiary. The hole seems to have been dug earlier. Even in the pitch dark, I can tell just by running my hands over the earth that it was dug at least a day ago. The earth has hardened like the blood on my face. Exposure to the elements has the same caking effect on freshly dug ground as it has on wounds. That's why they stopped.

Tomorrow, when the rightful recipient is interned, it will cover up their crime. They just needed to make sure that enough earth covered the hole so that I wasn't discovered. That means that I'm either at Riverview Memorial Park or the Washington State Cemetery.

One is in Riverview, and the other is a few miles outside of town. It's used mostly to bury people who cannot be identified. No one would think to look here for me—if they looked at all. If it is Washington State, at least the bordering forest will give me the cover I need to make my escape, especially if they're still here and I need to disappear into the woods.

I know these woods like the back of my hand, even though it's been years since I've been home. It takes me a few tries to get to the top of the hole. Thank you, rock climbing class and actual rock climbing. It's a bit tougher to peak out and survey the area. I can't see anything. On the plus side, I figure if I can't see them, then they can't see me.

I manage to crawl out of the hole and immediately know that I'm going to feel it in the morning. I lie still on the ground, letting the cold seep into my muscles. It's a balm for my body and helps me stay centered and plan my escape. I can't assume that they've left, but I do know that either way, I have to make my way to the woods.

I stay low and crawl. I wind my way through the graves with markers only containing numbers. It's heartbreaking, but I can't fixate on that right now. I need to keep moving. The pain from my head and right side is threatening to overcome me, but I keep moving. A thought tries to break through, but I can't seem to grab hold. I hear the thunder of running feet, and out of pure instinct, I hit the ground. A flashlight rolls across the ground like a lighthouse over the ocean, but instead of waves, there are rows of grave markers and mounds of freshly dug graves.

"She couldn't have gone far. Find her!"

The voice sounds vaguely familiar, but I can't place it right now.

"I told you to make sure she was dead! Just find her, you moron. I pay you a lot of money to make these sorts of problems go away!"

Problem!? How did I become a problem? What have I got myself mixed up in?

The footsteps are coming closer, and I can't risk just lying here. I have the dark on my side. I learned early on that the dark isn't to be feared. It could be my friend. Yes, bad things happen in the dark, but it can also be a weapon when you embrace it.

The flashlights multiply, and I count to get an idea of their intervals. Ten seconds. OK, I have to scramble every ten seconds and then lie flat, at least until I get to the woods. It's about a hundred feet. Go! I scramble frantically and hit the dirt a second before it hits me. I'm only a few feet from the edge of the woods. The scanning picks up pace, so I have to, too.

"Alex... Alex... let's talk about this..."

Where do I know that voice from? My mind is still grasping at random faces and images. Nothing is clear except that I have to get to safety. I don't even consider exactly where that is.

"You were safe in Boston! Miserable, yes, but safe!"

They're down to five seconds, and I realize that they know where I'm most likely headed. I decided to make a break for it before they got ahead of me and blocked my way to the forest. The dark and the forest are the only things that I have on my side. If I don't get lost in the foliage and trees and the dark, then I'm done for. I can't fight them. I'm too weak from blood loss and exhaustion.

My muscles are throbbing. I think something happened before I was knocked out. I don't even know what I'm up against. I may have a chance against one or two guys, but I don't know how many I'm facing. Best not to risk it. When the last beam strikes, I decide to just bolt for the last few feet until I'm enfolded by the forest. A beam catches me as I break through the doorway to the woods.

"I see you, Alex! Come back here!"

Has anyone ever responded to that and turned back? I keep running. I don't know yet which side of the woods I'm on. One side has the main entrance, the other three lead deeper into the forest, to the highway, and the third to the ocean.

My chest burns with the sheer exertion. I'm not a runner. I haven't been since I was a child, and I needed to run. I stop and lean against an elm tree. I try to quietly catch my breath, but it's hopeless. My body wants to take in great buckets full of air, and I can't help but wheeze.

The voices come closer, but not before I hear an oncoming car in the distance. I'm close to the highway. I can make a run for it and, hopefully, get help or safety. It's a long shot, especially this time of night. What if someone came to help them get rid of me? The thought stops me dead in my tracks. The truth is I don't know who I can trust. I don't know who's trying to kill me or why.

I decided that running towards the road is still my best bet, even if I just use it to get back to my room. I can't go back to my mom's house. I'd be putting her in danger, and I promised never to set foot there again. Ironic, given the fact that she's the reason I'm back here. If only I'd trusted my instinct and ignored that begging-for-help call. I decided to start running again.

"Go around. Don't let her get to the road!"

The voice is too close for comfort. I need to pick up the pace. I can't see very far ahead of me. The moon is full and bright. The clouds have parted, giving me just a sliver of light, but it's enough. I begin to give it all I've got as I head for the road. Suddenly, a huge figure looms in front of me.

"There you are."

I don't slow down. He tries to grab hold of me, but his size doesn't make him very agile. Instead, he tears a piece out of my favorite T-shirt. He loses his balance and hits the forest floor like a ton of bricks. I heave a sigh of relief that I didn't opt to fight.

I don't slow down and run through the pain, burning, and fatigue. I run because my life depends on it: if they catch me again, they'll make sure I'm dead before reburying me. I can't let that happen. It's difficult even with my knowledge of the forest floor and canopy, even with the moonlight and knowing where I'm headed.

The thunder of feet behind me is all but a distant noise, and I finally begin to hope that I might just make it out of this place again. How many lives does a cat have? Nine? *Please let me have another one*, I say to no one in particular.

My strength is about to give out on me, but the ground beats it to the punch. I'm rolling down the side of a hill. It's steep, and I know it well, but because I couldn't see far ahead, I missed it. I try to break my fall but only manage to slow myself down. I have no idea what I've hit or been slapped in the face with as I whirl my way through decaying branches, rocks, and foliage.

I eventually make it to the bottom and hear the thumping of feet above me. I don't have time to orient myself, and I try and get up, but something twisted or broken in my left arm and ankle. I struggle to get to my feet.

A car approaches. I can see the headlights, and I force myself to stand. I can't judge the distance. I don't even know if they'll stop and help or swerve around me, but I must try. I don't know how far I'll make it on a bum leg and how long it will take for them to catch me or another car to come. Deciding to take a chance, I limped towards the road.

My right eye is swollen shut, and I'm struggling to see out of the left one. All I see is the aura of the headlights as I step out onto the road, followed by the sound of wheels clawing at the tar to stop. Then the sound of metal hitting flesh and then air and then nothing.

I may not remember the last few hours but what I do know is that I'm getting close to finding out what exactly happened to Olivia and the others.

Vanishing Acts

Boston. Two months earlier.

The phone started buzzing the minute I let myself into my apartment. Tranquility destroyed. It's the phone I keep for my personal life, and only a handful of people have the number. I know I should answer, but there's no one that I particularly want to speak to right now. In fact—if I'm honest—answering this phone has only ever brought me heartache or trouble. I just didn't have the emotional bandwidth to deal with anything like that now.

I promised myself that when I got home, I would just focus on myself and rest. No drama. I've been being watched by the FBI for a few months now. My 'online activities' had struck them as suspicious, and I wasn't about to get dragged into anything else. I'd just been questioned for seven hours about everything from my childhood to my work. They wanted to know how I managed to live in this building on a corporate assistant's salary. Everything they could think of to get me to admit to being part of a group with 'known terrorist sympathies.'

It didn't matter that I worked as a paralegal for one of the city's most influential law firms. It was my computer science degree and my history of hacking that made me a person of interest. That and our firm's politically well-connected clients.

Terrorist, my eye. 'Ethical Hackers' were anything but terrorist sympathizers, but ever since they'd exposed high-profile politicians and their corrupt dealings, they'd been in the FBI's crosshairs. I'd been placed on 'special leave' pending the outcome of their investigation.

The only reason I was still being paid was to keep up the front of not 'victimizing' me and unintentionally making me a martyr. It was also to keep my mouth shut. Not that they'd said so, but I'm smarter than I pretend to be. They suspended my company access, and I couldn't even log in remotely to access emails. Not that I would, but it spoke volumes.

I went to the bathroom and after a shower, I ran a comb through my reddish-brown hair and then added eye drops to my Hazel colored almond-shaped eyes. They are red from not sleeping properly. I touched my face and my skin looked paler than usual. I considered putting on make-up but decided against it.

The phone started buzzing again, and I decided that as soon as it stopped, I would turn it off. Just rest and relax. I wasn't about to check who was so insistent on getting hold of me. I just couldn't be bothered. The press had been having a field day. My apartment building was surrounded, and I just needed to hunker down and ride it out. I'd probably have to move as soon as I was cleared.

I looked in the refrigerator and took out a couple of free-range eggs, shallots, cheese, and red, yellow, and green peppers. I took a couple of slices of sourdough bread out to toast. I turned on the TV and flipped through the channels while I waited for the pan to heat. I had just tossed a sliver of butter into the olive oil and added some Himalayan salt and ground pepper to the oil when I saw my building appear on the news.

I let out an exasperated sigh and cracked the eggs into a bowl. I beat them too hard and spilled some over the side and onto the marble countertops. I glanced around, and although the place was relatively small and compact, I had to admit that the FBI's interest was justified. A look into my finances would reveal nothing out of the ordinary, even to a trained eye.

My explanation would hold up to the most intense scrutiny. The truth usually did. My aunt Bella had left it to me. She was the first in our family to put an entire continent between her and my family. I never did know how Bella made her money. I just know she and my mom were like night and day. She loved life and lived it at 120mph. "Never fall in love, my love," she'd said to me countless times. "Men will break you." She didn't have to tell me that; I had learned that early.

I couldn't tell her that; she would have flown home to Riverview and shot my stepdad. She had a gun. She'd shown it to me dozens of times. A figure came into view on the screen, and I was called back to the reality I was living and away from the fun and safe summers with Bella. It was the doorman, Nigel. He was being interviewed. I turned the volume up. Nigel had been the doorman since my aunt Bella lived here. He was the only man I'd ever trusted. I turned the sound up.

"You people need to leave that poor young girl alone. She's like a daughter to me. I've known her since she was this high." He indicated to his mid-thigh.

"She's a good girl. Never gives her aunt a day's trouble!"

He was emotional and struggling to keep it together.

"Why don't you go and question those fat cats about why they're picking on her."

I wanted to run downstairs and tell him it was okay, but that would only fuel the fire. Besides, he was handling himself well—better than I did when the tsunami of flashing bulbs first hit me a few months before.

I turned off the set and returned to making myself something to eat. I didn't have much of an appetite, but I knew that I needed to eat. I hadn't eaten in a few days, and I was running on fumes. My sleep had never been the best, but these last few months had been worse than usual.

For some reason, I was being singled out by the FBI. The other hackers—or suspected hackers—had long since gotten out of dodge and been cleared. As was the code, we all went to the ground and cut off any contact. We knew what to do in situations like this.

In the age of information as currency, hackers were the dealers du jour. Some used their abilities for good and to cast a spotlight on crime and injustices, and others just worked to line their pockets or for the highest bidder. The irony was that, in the Senator Adler case, I had nothing to do with any of it. My name had just popped up, as it always seems to when intricate hacking activities come to light. Not that I was upset about it, but something about this seemed different.

I was finishing up the omelets and had just popped the bread in to get it nice and golden brown when I heard a ruckus outside.

"Get outta here before I call the cops."

I took the pan off the stove and popped the toast before cleaning my hands and going to see what the commotion was about.

Nigel was on the outside, just a few doors down, trying to get a man out of the corridor. The man was resisting, and neither of them noticed that they had an audience as other residents came to see what was going on.

"Miss Harper... just a few minutes of your time. Trig Atkins from the Boston Standard. Please, people want to know your side of the story. Just give me a few minutes, and this all goes away. "

"Yeah, right!" I thought.

Nigel turned. "Go inside, Alex. I've got this." I did as I was told.

Nigel returned a few minutes later. I invited him in for a cup of coffee.

"Anything stronger?"

I poured him some bourbon. My aunt loved it, and Nigel loved it. I kept it for when he popped around to check on me—a promise he'd made to my aunt before she died. He always kept it. We sat quietly for a while. Neither of us spoke.

"Is the front door covered?" I didn't want to get him into any more trouble.

"I'm not in any trouble," he said, smiling at me.

"How..." He could always read my thoughts.

"You're just like your aunt. Good people. I know you're not mixed up in any of this. I'm just sorry I let that guy get so close."

"Don't beat yourself up. It was bound to happen. They're like piranha scenting blood. They're just doing their jobs, I suppose."

"Yeah, well that doesn't make it right. In my day we had scandals, but they were still respectful... this new lot are just a bunch of fucking animals." He blushed.

"Sorry, Ally cat!" The childhood nickname warmed me up and took me back to better, happier times.

"It's okay. I know you're looking out for me."

He gave me a pet name as soon as we met, and I loved it. Once I was comfortable around him and trusted him, we became close very quickly. I still didn't call him by his first name, though. It seemed too impersonal.

"I'll leave you to it, my angel." He handed me back the glass.

"The door waits for no one." That was his parting joke for as long as I'd known him. Then he turned to look at me, and he seemed a little sad.

"I'm sure you've noticed that I don't stay here very long anymore...." He didn't wait for me to answer. "It's not you. I just want you to know that."

"I know, Uncle Nige." I hugged him and heard him sniff.

"I just still miss her so much."

It was the first time he'd admitted it to me. I'd always had a sense that there was more to their relationship or that he wanted more—I don't know which, but neither one had admitted it to me. Even when I asked as a young girl, they would just catch each other's gaze and smile. A secret smile.

"Look at me. A fool to behave like this at my age." I just squeezed his arm reassuringly.

"Promise me that you'll take care of yourself, Ally cat. Don't make me live through losing you too. You're all I have left of her."

"I promise. I'm not involved in any of this, I swear."

"I know."

He turned and opened the door, and just like that, I was alone again. I decided to do one thing he asked and look after myself. I finished off my early dinner and started running a soothing bath for myself. Lavender, vanilla, and sea salt, just as Aunt Bella taught me., and then to top it off, her special rosemary, mint, and chamomile tea oil infusion. The warm water was like a balm for my soul. The fragrances had the desired effect, and I could feel myself unwinding.

I never took medication, but I thought a sleeping pill would do me a world of good under the circumstances. I temporarily rethought it as I nursed the last of the white wine from dinner. I decided on half. When my body was sufficiently relaxed, and every muscle had turned to exquisite jelly, I got out and rinsed off in the shower. I took five minutes to wash my hair and apply some leave-in conditioner. The smell was so heavenly that for a few minutes, everything seemed all right. I dried myself off and changed into my favorite pair of cotton PJs. The kittens on the material always made me feel contented. How something as simple as playing with yarn can bring such joy has always fascinated and inspired me.

I took a glass of water and the sleeping tablet to the bedroom and put it on the side of the bed. It was still light out, and I closed the drapes, padded across the warm wooden floors, and curled into bed. Swallowing the tablet. I drifted off into the peaceful oblivion that is sleep.

Cryptic Clues

The pounding on the front door roused me from a deep and dreamless sleep. I didn't know how much time has passed, but I was pissed off by whoever had disturbed my sleep. The pounding stopped when I turned on the light in the entryway.

Someone slipped a postcard underneath the door, and by the time I opened the front door, they'd vanished. I strained to look both ways down the passage and saw no one. My mind drifted back to the reporter from earlier, and I kicked myself for even opening the. Truth be told, I thought it was the FBI again. They'd torn the place apart twice, looking for anything that could link me to Ethical Hackers, but had come up empty.

It wasn't like in the movies. They leave a mess, and you have to clean it up. Break things and empty out even sugar containers and freezers looking for evidence. I guess I should have been thankful that they didn't plant anything. I closed the door and made sure to lock it behind me before I turned off the light. Then I remembered the postcard, and I turned the light back on and picked up the card.

It didn't occur to me to use gloves. I couldn't make out the message; it was some kind of code. Not computer code but a combination of symbols and Greek or Roman letters. When I turned it over, the picture startled me. It was from my hometown of Riverview but not today or even this decade. Riverview 1996. The year before I was born.

I was born the next year during the centenary of the founding of the town. The strange thing was that I'd never seen this postcard. Aunt Bella had collected all the postcards from that year and the year of my birth before she moved to Boston. She didn't like to talk about that time except to say it was the happiest and saddest of her life. I just figured that it was when she'd had her heart broken.

The postcard captured two people, a man and a woman who were clearly in love, on the banks of Lake River, for which the town is named. People had speculated that it was named after the Rivers family, who had founded the town and whose estate could be seen from anywhere in the town.

By the time I was born, the town had become a haven for the growing IT millionaires and billionaires. The locals were just happy to be spared the fate of other towns that were dying out as young people flocked to Seattle to be a part of the tech boom. Many of the families still lived or vacationed there. Many would drive the two hours from Seattle to spend weekends there because despite its proximity and modern amenities it still retained its small-town feel.

I never would have left if I hadn't been driven out. The couple on the banks of the river weren't picnicking or posing for the picture. It was clearly clandestine, and there was something familiar about them. The man's face was turned away from the camera. I turned off the light and went back to bed, leaving the postcard on the kitchen counter.

I battled to get back to sleep. I didn't dare look at the time because I knew it would just make me more anxious. Besides, the postcard kept bothering me. I decided to get up and make myself some warm milk with honey and cinnamon to get back to sleep. I willed myself to ignore the postcard, and eventually, I threw it in the trash.

I went to the sofa curled my feet underneath me, and sipped on the warm, sweet concoction. As the liquid wound its way through me, I began to feel more at ease. Feeling a little safer now, I allowed myself to go onto the balcony and just stare up. I loved stargazing as a child. I started noticing patterns in the stars even before I knew what astronomy was. It was my Aunt Bella and Nigel who saw my drawings and realized that I was drawing constellations.

Finding patterns in seemingly random things fascinated me. Puzzles give me a sense of control over a world that seemed out of control. By the time I was nine, I was assembling complicated puzzles. My latest obsession was 3D puzzles. I've already completed the Sistine Chapel and the Notre Dame. I was currently working on the Eiffel

Tower or had been before all this happened. The half-finished tower mocked me from beside the television. I turned to look at it and then went back to the stars.

I was in no mood for puzzles or mysteries. I couldn't even figure out how I'd landed up in the center of this mess. I finished the milk and decided to give sleep another try. I rinsed the mug and put it back in the cupboard, and then, on sheer impulse, I retrieved the postcard from the bin. I still hadn't figured anything out, but it dawned on me that one of my friends may have left it as a clue to what the hell was going on.

I went to the sofa and turned the TV on. The background noise always greased the wheels of my brain. I wasn't one of those people who needed complete silence to think. The busier and noisier my surroundings were, the better. The upside of childhood trauma. I don't think I even understood the power of quiet until I began to spend summers here in Boston.

I was staring at the Greek symbols and noticed that it was a sorority. Phi Beta Delta. I hadn't come across that since... before high school graduation. All the popular girls at my school were talking about going off to Ivy League colleges and pledging to the same sorority—that way, no matter where they ended up, they'd always be sisters.

That was around the time Diana Chase and Meredith Lynch had disappeared. It was a horrible time. Girls walked around in packs or at least in twos if their parents or their staff even let them out. It seemed to be only girls from well-to-do families disappearing. Us townies weren't concerned.

Olivia! Wow. I hadn't thought about her in years. I was the only person she felt safe with—she asked me to go everywhere with her. When she headed to California to attend Stanford University, I came to live with my aunt and worked my way through Boston College. We kept in touch for a little while, but eventually, life overtook us. The last time we spoke, she was engaged and moving to San Francisco.

She pledged Phi Beta Delta. That seemed weird. I went to fetch a pencil from the kitchen junk drawer and went back to the sofa. I drew a rectangle around the sorority letters and then tried to figure out what the rest meant. I could feel something itching to emerge from somewhere in the recesses of my brain, but I couldn't quite put my finger on it. I don't know how long I was at it, but I decided to rest my eyes after a while.

I woke up with a start hours later. The sun's rays were inching their way across the floor. I turned off the TV. I went to the bathroom, tied my hair up and splashed cold water on my face. I brushed my teeth and then decided to make myself some coffee. I'd just turned on the machine when there was another knock at the door. I looked through the keyhole and saw the night shift doorman, Hector.

"Morning, Hector," I said, opening the door.

"Morning, Miss Harper. My apologies for disturbing you, but Nigel said not to leave any packages downstairs. These were just delivered for you." He handed me the box.

"Do you know who delivered this, Hector? There's no label or waybill on it."

I eyed the package suspiciously before taking it from him. He seemed nervous, but I chalked it up to having to come upstairs to deliver a package, which was, strictly speaking, against the rules.

"It was a man, but his face was hidden by his baseball cap. Early too. Just after 6 am." He left, obviously not wanting to get involved with whatever was going on.

I decided to play it safe and call the special agent in charge of the investigation. It might not have been related, but I didn't want to get in any more trouble. What if there was a snake or bomb in the package? Was I just being paranoid? I took a deep breath and then decided to go with my first instinct.

Special Agent Du Val was there in five minutes, partly because he probably wasn't far away to begin with. I guess anything that could help him wrap up this case was a good thing. I let him in immediately.

"What do you think it is?" he asked.

I stared at him, bewildered. "I don't know. That's why I called you."

"Look, either way, it doesn't matter. I was on my way here to tell you that you are no longer a person of interest in the investigation."

"Since when?"

"Order came from up high. Last night. Interpol nabbed some guy in Paris." He didn't look particularly happy.

"Anyway, you and your parcels and postcards are no longer any business of the bureau." He said the last part with more than a little disdain in his voice.

"So that's it. You guys cost me my job and turned my life upside down for months and then just... oops, I'm on my own?" I was livid.

"It's nothing pers..."

I couldn't take another word. "Oh, shut up and get out."

I stormed over to the door and opened it. I was about to let it all out, and I'd be damned if I did it in front of this condescending bastard. To his credit, he left quietly and quickly. But before I could close the door, he yelled over his shoulder.

"Answer your phone. A detective out in Riverview is trying to get ahold of you."

I could sense the smirk on his face without even looking at him. He was happy that I seemed to be headed for more trouble.

I got into the shower and turned it on cold, screaming as the ice-cold stream hit my warm skin. And then I just kept screaming to let it all out. Thankfully this was a corner apartment, and there was no one on the other side of the bathroom wall. The cold water gave way to salty tears, and then I just surrendered to it.

Months of harassment and questioning at all hours of the day and night and all the while I'd convinced myself that I was fine. I was just running through the debris. Trying not to face any of it. When I cried out, I put on a robe and made my way back to the kitchen. I turned the phone back on, but just the thought of what awaited me on the other end of the line made my chest tighten, so I just went to my still-dark room and crawled back into bed. The soft crisp linen and pillows cradled me like a hug. The smell of lavender and vanilla still lingered on the sheets and soothed me. My eyes and cheeks were still painful from crying, but it worked better than a dozen sleeping tablets. Free now of the worry and anxiety, I just drifted off again.

Unlikely Alliance

When I awoke, it felt like I'd been sleeping for a century. My limbs even felt weak, like the atrophy that sets in for coma patients. It took me a few minutes and loads of stretching before I wanted to get out of bed. I had to fight the impulse to go back to bed. I gave myself some time to acclimate to my new normal. After making myself some coffee, I decided to put on some fresh clothing. I considered going for a walk, but unsure if the media were still camped outside, I decided to call the front desk. Nigel answered.

"Great news about the FBI clearing you, hey, Ally cat?" I breathed a sigh of relief. It wasn't just a fantasy.

"Yes, it's wonderful, Uncle Nige. I don't know what to do with myself now. Are the reporters still outside?"

"No. Those clowns took off minutes after the FBI reported that you'd been cleared. Didn't even wait for a comment from you." I smiled at how protective he still remained.

"I wouldn't have had anything to say anyway. It doesn't feel real yet."

"Well, it is. Thank God." He seemed happier about it than me. "You get out there and start living again. Go get some coffee, maybe something to eat. Feel the sunshine on your face. Breathe in the fresh air. I'm headed out."

"Out? What time is it?"

"It's after 6, angel. Time for me to head home. Hectors just arrived."

"I don't suppose you have time for a cup of coffee with me. Maybe dinner?"

"I'd love to."

Spending some time with him always perked me up. He was the one constant from my childhood aside from Aunt Bella. It was three years since she died, and neither one of us had the guts to acknowledge just how different the world was without her. I threw myself into my work with Ethical Hackers. Anger and grief are a terrible combination but a fierce motivator. Losing someone you love so young—possibly the only person who truly loved you—does something to a person. I never thought about it until now, but he must have been feeling it too. I was at work, and he was there. He told me they'd just been chatting, and she said she was going to the corner store to get some things to make my favorite dish. She asked him to come to dinner, and then she was gone. He didn't know something had happened until he heard the sirens.

"Great. I'll be down in a few minutes."

"Okay, I'll change into my civilian clothes."

I laughed for the first time in months. Aunt Bella had mentioned that he'd been in the army—fought in the Gulf—but he didn't like to talk about it, and "You're not to ask questions, Alex!". I could still hear her voice in my head. I think she had wanted to be an actress or a writer. She had a way of carrying herself and speaking that you only see in actors. She could read people in seconds and empathize with anyone. She was extraordinary. Although Uncle Nige always told me I reminded him of her, I know he's only being kind. I didn't have her way with people, her kindness, and her ability to connect. I felt safer in the online world than in the real one.

Uncle Nigel and I went to the coffee shop two blocks over. They made a great BLT, and he and I both loved it. He's really thoughtful and considerate. He and Aunt Bella complemented each other well.

"Did you love her?"

He didn't look up from his sandwich. "Very much."

He didn't elaborate, and I didn't pry. We just sat in contented silence, enjoying our food. It was as though I'd never tasted food before. Even the cranberry crush, my all-time favorite on the menu, tasted like I was having it for the first time. In truth, it was probably my ten thousandth cup. Tea and cranberry juice blended together with a dollop of cream. Heaven.

"I'm sorry about your friend."

I looked up at him, startled. "My friend?"

"Yes. The one from Riverview. She came to visit for a few days one summer. Olivia something?"

"Sinclair?"

"Yes." He took another bite but stopped mid-chew. "Oh, fuck. Sorry, love. You probably haven't been watching much TV."

"What happened?"

He was sheepish now, reluctant to be the bearer of more bad news. "She's gone missing. She was home from California. Staying with her folks. She told them she was going out, and they hadn't seen or heard from her in days."

"That agent told me a detective from Riverview was trying to get hold of me, but I haven't been answering my phone. I thought it was my mother."

I saw him wince but ignored it. I knew that he and Aunt Bella suspected things weren't right back home but didn't know what to do because I refused to talk about it.

I'd lost my appetite. I wiped my mouth and tossed the napkin on the plate.

"What are you going to do?" He looked at me nervously.

"I don't know. Call him and find out what's going on, I guess. " I shrugged my shoulders because I didn't know what to do.

"Like Bella used to say, there's nothing to do until there's something that needs doing."

He seemed satisfied with that, and it set my mind at ease, too. He was right. I didn't know what was going on, and until I did, it was best not to get myself worked up.

"We can head back if you want to call him."

"I hate cutting our dinner short." I knew he would be able to see that I was genuinely sorry, but he also knew me well enough to know that I wouldn't rest until I got an answer.

"It's fine, Ally cat. It won't be our last." He looked down, and I knew that there was something he wanted to say.

"What's wrong, Uncle Nige? What is it?"

"Please, kiddo... promise me one thing?"

"What?"

"Whatever your friend's gotten mixed up in, don't get drawn into it."

"I won't. I promise. I've had my share of drama to last a lifetime."

I was convinced that I wouldn't be dragged into whatever was happening with Olivia. She pulled these kinds of stunts all the time in school. Her home life was almost as bad as mine. Then something happened in our senior year, just before we all left for college, and she was just different.

"You say that now, but I know you, Ally."

Uh oh. He dropped the *cat*. He was really concerned. He'd never been stern with me unless he saw that I was headed down a dangerous path or making a bad decision, usually with boys. He'd been right every single time.

"I promise, Uncle Nige. No getting drawn back to Riverview." That seemed to placate him. He knew one thing—that I would never willingly lie to him or break a promise to him.

"For either of us."

"What do you mean?"

He looked caught off guard.

"I thought your aunt told you. I grew up in Riverview."

"No. She never said anything. You grew up in Riverview too!?" I can't believe it. "Wow, it's a small world, isn't it?"

"Not really. We knew each other back home. It took me a while, but I eventually worked up the courage to follow her here. Once I knew where she was."

"Why did she move here? She never told me."

He seemed caught off guard by the question. "We'll talk about it the next time we have dinner. For now, I think you'd better put your mind at ease about your friend."

He was right, of course. History could wait. I needed to speak to the detective from Riverview and see how I could help, if at all.

"I'll get dinner. You stay and eat. See you tomorrow."

I got up before he could protest. He was old school and would want to pay for the meal, but I caught him between mouthfuls of potato salad. I dropped a twenty on the table and left before he could protest. It was no minor feat, considering he was a former military man, and they're known for their quick reflexes.

I walked back to the building and, out of habit, checked my mailbox. It was near bursting point. I hadn't checked in for at least a week. While I waited for the elevator, I threw away the junk mail and cards from journalists, which thinned the pile significantly. When the elevator reached the ground floor, two older women got off and nodded politely. I didn't know them, but they'd lived here at least as long as I had. I waited for them to exit before getting on and pressing the button for the eighth floor.

I'd caught some of what they'd been talking about: my recent troubles. But I couldn't be bothered to care. The elevator made its way slowly to my floor. Mail forgotten, I prayed that it didn't stop for anyone else. I didn't have the energy to deal with people. I just needed to get back to my apartment and lock the world out. It had been great getting out and spending time with Uncle Nige, but now I was feeling... it was almost as though being outside made me feel claustrophobic. Weird. I had never been an introvert who hated the outdoors: actually, I was quite the opposite. I loved the freedom of the outdoors. It had always been a safe place for me. I couldn't be trapped or cornered outdoors.

The elevator dinged when it reached my floor, and I practically sprinted out. I had my keys at the ready. It was another thing I never bothered with before. Usually, I would take my keys out when it dawned on me that I needed to get inside. In those unencumbered days, I could be oblivious and free. The fight or flight mode was permanently switched off. It was a long time in the making, and it was glorious. Then Aunt Bella died, and in the last few months, I was like an addict backsliding. The same drug that had numbed me and kept me alive now felt like a poison to my system.

I let myself in quickly and went to pick up my phone, scrolling through the missed calls and the voice messages. I decided the messages were my best bet: no trolling through a list of numbers. The first few messages were from work and journalists. How in the hell did they get this number? There was a couple from my mother. I hit save or delete as I saw fit until I got to the one, I was looking for, from Detective Adrian Miller. He didn't say anything in the message except to call him.

"Miller." His response when he answered my call was so terse that I hesitated for a few seconds before answering.

"Detective Miller, it's Alex Harper. Alexandra Harper."

"Ms. Harper. It is Ms., isn't it?"

"Yes, but please call me Alex."

"Ms. Harper, I'm calling in connection with the disappearance of your friend Olivia Sinclair. Is it possible for you to come in and answer a few questions that will aid in our investigation?

"I don't know how much help I'd be. I haven't spoken to Olivia in a few years. We lost touch after she said she was getting married and moving to San Francisco."

"Married?"

"Yes. She said she'd met some guy who was going to change the world and was in IT. The next Bill Gates. They were going to move there because he worked in Silicon Valley. That was the last time we spoke."

"We have no record of her being married or even engaged. She dropped out of college and was living with her parents didn't you think it was strange that she didn't send you an invite to her wedding or never got in touch after that?"

"I didn't think about it. We were so different by the time we left high school that I was surprised that we kept in touch as long as we did. I'd moved to Boston and had a life here, and I figured it was just one of those things."

"What do you mean, you were both so different when you left high school?"

"People grow. Things happen." It wasn't an answer, but it was the best I could do. "How does high school have anything to do with her disappearance?"

"I don't know, Ms. Harper. It seems that she got stuck there for some reason. You were the closest person to her during those years, at least according to her parents. They seem to think that you might be able to help us figure this thing out."

"I'm not sure I can, Detective. I don't even know if I can go back there. It's just... I'm sorry, I have to go." I ended the call and turned off the phone.

High school was such a long time ago, and yet sometimes it felt like it was just yesterday. Why did Olivia lie? Did she just up an entire life? It was mind-boggling. I left the mail on the counter and crawled onto the sofa. I turned on the TV to drown out my thoughts.

The missed clues. What had I missed? What couldn't she tell me? I knew I had my secrets, but it never dawned on me that she had hers too. I got up, got some sparkling water from the fridge, and poured myself a glass. I popped a couple of sleeping tablets into my mouth without a second thought. Making my way to the bedroom, I slowly undressed and threw my clothing over the wing-backed leather chair in the corner. It was the only use that chair seemed to have. I crawled between the sheets and drifted off.

That had been my routine for a couple of days. I barely ate. I knew that at some point, Uncle Nige would come check on me. I wanted to set his mind at ease, but the only thing that I was capable of was sleep.

When the knock came, I tried my best not to sound groggy. "I'm coming, just a second." Even I wasn't convinced by my attempt. I splashed cold water on my face and tied my brown hair in a scrunchy on top of my head. I tossed a capful of mouthwash into my mouth and swirled it about before spitting it out.

I got to the door just after the second knock. "I'm coming, Uncle Nige."

"I've been called a lot of things, but that's new even for me." The bright bushy bushy-tailed man on the other side of the door was not Uncle Nige.

"Ms. Harper?"

"Yes."

He extended his hand. I took it, still confused, and then panicked, thinking another reporter had sneaked into the building.

"Adrian Miller. Detective Miller." He stumbled over his words. I realized as he was averting his eyes because I hadn't put on a robe and answered the door in my T-shirt and underwear.

"Detective Miller. Oh my god, I thought it was a friend. I'm so sorry." I tried to cover myself, but my hands didn't quite do the trick." I bolt to the bedroom yelling "Come in" over my shoulder.

Dangerous Connections

When I came back, he was still waiting at the door.

"Please come in, Detective." He moved toward me and then took a seat at the counter. He seemed uneasy.

"What are you doing in Boston, long way from your jurisdiction, no?"

"I'm sorry to barge in on you like this... I did try to call." He sounded apologetic. "When you wouldn't respond, my chief authorized me to fly out here and meet you face to face."

"It's okay, but like I already told you on the phone, I don't know how I can help you."

Something softened in his face, and I could see that he was sizing me up. He couldn't think that I had anything to do with Olivia's disappearance, but he did believe that it was tied to our time in high school.

"We ran a check on her phone records, and it seems she placed several calls to you in the days leading up to her disappearance. We know they weren't long enough to have any real conversations, but did she leave you any messages?"

"I don't know... I haven't been checking my messages," I replied sheepishly. "But then you know that already."

Now it was his turn to look sheepish, but he just powered through. "Have you had a chance to since we spoke?"

"No, I haven't ...in fact, I turned it off again." I couldn't quite look him in the eye.

"Yeah, I know. " He looked at the ground and then out the window. "I don't think your friend is dead, but I do think she's in danger." He caught my startled gaze. "I'm sorry. I didn't mean to be so blunt. It's just we're chasing our tails on this one, and I'd rather solve a missing person's case than a murder."

"I'm sorry. It never dawned on me that it could be this serious. Something happened in high school... I think maybe two things. That's when she started disappearing and being secretive. She'd always come back and then one day she came back, and she was just different."

"Different how?"

I could see his interest was piqued.

"I don't know. Like shell-shocked. That's the best way I can describe it. I tried to ask her about it, but she would just avoid the question until one day she became hysterical and screamed at me that if I ever asked her again, she'd stop being my friend. So I stopped, and she stopped being my friend anyway."

"I thought you said that you guys still kept in touch after high school."

"We did, but it wasn't the same... Like she was weaning herself off me. I don't know. She was always busy and avoided me like the plague but still kept in touch, messaging and all that... and then one day it was the last time we spoke." I got up and asked him if he wanted something to drink.

"Coffee?" It was both a question and a statement.

"Sure." I turned on the coffee machine and then got my phone. When the coffee as done, I took it to him with cream and sugar.

While he stirred his coffee, I accessed the voice messages on my phone. I put it on speaker. There were dozens of messages. I hit save or delete as each one popped up. He listened to some intently and dismissed others.

"Don't delete the ones when no one speaks." That was all he said. This went on for nearly half an hour until Olivia's voice crackled to life. It startled me.

"Hi there, stranger. I bet I'm the last person you thought would call you out of the blue." There was a pause, and then the sound of lockers slamming and a faint echo. *"I'm just taking a walk down memory lane. I can't live with it anymore. I should have spoken to you when I had the*

chance, and now it's too late." There was a sudden buzzing sound, and she screamed. The call ended.

I started screaming and crying. I couldn't help it.

"Oh my god, oh my god, Olivia! I screamed at the phone, wishing she would somehow appear out of it like a genie from a lamp.

A moment later, there was a knock at the door. He rushed to let whomever it was in. I ran to Uncle Nige when he walked in. I could barely speak. "Someone's hurt her. Oh god, it's my fault.... why didn't I answer her call..."

"It's OK, angel. It's OK."

I sobbed until I thought I had no more tears left, and then I sobbed some more.

It took me a while to get it together. Detective Miller just sat there, not knowing what to do. Eventually, I composed myself. This wasn't doing me or Olivia any good. I needed to go to Riverview.

"How can I help? Do you still want me to come to Riverview?" I didn't look at Uncle Nige because I knew what he'd say.

"Ally..."

"I have to... please understand."

"Then I'm coming too."

"I can't ask you to do that."

"You didn't. Besides, we all have demons to face back home."

"I'm not sure. This is difficult for you."

"I've already survived difficult. I'll be fine. If you don't need my help I'll go back on my own!"

Catching sight of the postcard on the coffee table, Uncle Nige sees it and turns white.

"What's this?" He picked it up as though it was a poisonous spider.

"Someone shoved it under the door a few nights ago. I called the FBI, but they said it didn't concern them. It was 'my problem.'" I looked at his face. "What's wrong? You look as though you've seen a ghost."

"I have... my own..."

"What?" I couldn't make out what he was trying to say.

"This is me and your Aunt Bella... the year before you were born."

I was speechless, overwhelmed by too much information. I'd just found out a few days ago that he was from Riverview, and now this. It was just too much.

"Why did you two never say anything?" I realized that his eyes were full of tears. Even though I was angry, I still felt for him.

"She asked me not to. Made me promise." His tears fell on the postcard, and he used his shirt to wipe them away as if he couldn't stand for her photograph to be damaged.

I reached out my hand to comfort him, and forgiveness was implied. We held each other for a while.

"I guess we all have secrets and promises to keep." I hugged him again. "You'll tell me when you're able to. Right now, I need to find out what happened to my friend."

Detective Miller shifted uncomfortably. "I don't think that will be necessary, Miss Archer."

"I wasn't asking permission, Detective."

I was tired, and I was done running, hiding, and being bullied and messed with. I may not have been able to deal with my own life right then, but obviously, this had something to do with me, Olivia, Uncle Nige, and Aunt Bella. I just didn't know what yet. But the way I saw it, it was a puzzle, and if there was one thing I was good at, it was figuring out things.

Everything had a logic and a reason. It often came down to one thing, one simple piece of the equation. I took the postcard from Uncle Nige and picked my phone up. I got up and went to the bedroom to pack a few things, but not before scooping up the mail on the counter. I might as well get some reading done on the plane. I steeled my nerves and told myself that this was all going to be just fine. I couldn't have been more wrong if I tried.

Interloper

I tucked my meager possessions into the overhead compartment and settled in for the trip. In a million years, I never would have guessed that I'd be heading back to Riverview. My thoughts drifted to Olivia and the voicemail she'd left on my phone. How did she get my number? There was something else, and I was struggling to move the fog surrounding it away. It seemed right there, just out of my reach. When I figured it out, I'd probably kick myself.

As the flight took off, I pulled my sketch pad out of my purse and started doodling. My phone wasn't an option, even though I was dying to listen to the rest of the messages. I was pretty sure that I'd erased most of the ones from the press, but to be honest, the ones I was avoiding were from my mother.

I was convinced Olivia and the others had got my number from her. Aunt Bella warned me about letting her have it, but I didn't want to listen. I guess it was the little girl inside me hoping that she would one day call and ask for forgiveness or even just explain why she seemed to hate me so much. I was so lost in thought that I didn't notice Detective Miller and Uncle Nige make their way to the vacant seats beside me.

"How're ya holding up, kiddo?"

I glanced up from the sketch pad and looked into his eyes. I didn't realize just how anxious I was until I looked at him and felt safe.

"I'm OK."

"Liar." He gave me one of his Santa Claus chuckles, the sound as reassuring as always. "Don't worry. Everything's going to be fine. I'm here, and I'll die before I let anyone hurt you."

"You know me so well."

"Look, I know that you're scared to death about going back there, and understandably so. Your life there was hell. No exaggeration."

"Hell would have been a vacation in comparison."

"Sometimes, for whatever reason, our lives have terrible beginnings and happy endings or vice versa. No one knows why, but if you learn early to live in the moments of joy, no matter what storm surrounds you, everything looks different. Riverview is a wonderful place. Great people. Beautiful lakes, woods, and wide-open spaces. Don't let the abuse from your mom and the string of bastards that she went through rob you of that joy. You've grown into an amazing, strong, and resilient young woman. They couldn't stop that from happening. You won, honey. They didn't."

I don't know why, but I threw myself into his arms. It surprised us both. While he was generous with his affection, I tended to be more controlled. I didn't know where it stemmed from.

Sometimes I had dreams from my childhood. A woman's face, laughing and loving me. I felt so happy and safe in the dreams... I felt loved. I knew it was not my mom. It seemed like a wish more than a memory, but it felt so real. I didn't even know how old I was in the dream, but I knew that I was loved. I pulled away from Uncle Nige and blinked away tears.

"It's OK, you know," he said.

"What?"

"To be afraid and hopeful and feel all those crazy confusing emotions all at once."

I inhaled deeply to calm myself, but it didn't help. He'd hit the nail on the head. As if to help me find my way out of my tangled web of thoughts, he glanced at the sketchpad and changed the subject.

"I haven't seen you with one of these since..."

"Since Aunt Bella died?"

"I didn't want to say it, but yes."

He stared at the doodles and, as usual, tried to make sense of them. They looked like a series of numbers and symbols, but experience had taught him that they weren't.

"OK, Einstein. What is it?" He slaps his forehead with his palm. "Oh man, do I ever regret giving you that book about the first female cryptkeepers!"

I burst into laughter. He never could get their names or professions right. "Cryptologists. Agnes Meyer Driscoll and Genevieve Grotjan Feinstein."

"OK, but to be fair, not many people can remember that."

"That's because, like most trailblazing women, history buried them in favor of celebrating the men who stole their work."

He nodded in agreement. We'd had this conversation many times before. He was the first one to realize my aptitude for solving puzzles, riddles, and equations. It started one night when I was five, he told me. He and Aunt Bella had gotten stuck on a 1000-piece puzzle and gotten blotto instead. She went to bed, and he passed out on the sofa. When they woke up, it was finished. They assumed they'd just been too drunk to remember finishing it.

Then one day, he'd taken me with him to Hayes Market to buy a couple of lottery tickets and pick up a few things for Aunt Bella's world-famous chicken parm lasagna. Two things happened: first, I asked him if I could pick the numbers, and he reluctantly agreed. I stood in front of the board for nearly an hour, studying the previous winning numbers. I never said anything to him, but for some reason even though I still didn't understand, I could see patterns in the numbers. I picked three lines, and he played them, along with his usual numbers, of course. He wasn't going to trust a five-year-old with his jackpot.

When we got to the register with items for Aunt Bella, I added up the total before the till. The cashier was impressed but thought it was a trick and then pointed out that I had calculated a dollar short. I promptly replied, "No. You didn't take into account that the chicken, parmesan, and canned tomatoes are on special." Uncle Nige couldn't wait to tell Aunt Bella, who promptly lifted me up and swung me around.

"I knew there was a reason I loved you from the moment you were born."

Later that night the two of them eagerly watched the lottery draw. It was their weekly ritual. I'd gone to sleep long back and was probably playing with Wendy, Peter Pan, or Tinkerbell in my dreams. The screaming ripped me out of my sleep, and for a moment, I was back in Riverview in that tiny little house at the end of the dirt road. Even then, the panic would overtake me. I started crying, and they must have realized what had happened because they were in the room like a flash, both on the verge of tears.

"Oh baby, we're so sorry. We didn't mean to scare you. The most exciting thing happened."

"What?" I managed through the sobs.

"The numbers you chose with Uncle Nige. All three lines had winning numbers, honey. It's unbelievable." Their eyes danced with delight.

"Are we rich?" I started dreaming of toys and more puzzles than I could ever finish.

"No, not rich, but we won't have to worry about money for a while, and you will have a nice little nest egg when you grow up." Uncle Nige was beside himself, and Aunt Bella just looked relieved.

When I woke up the next day, I thought it had all just been a dream, but after a few days, we all went off to large lawyers' offices, and they set up a trust. It was only when I was in college and the first checks came that I knew that the trust was for me, not them. They'd always sworn me to secrecy, probably knowing that my mother would waste any of the money before I turned eight if she knew about it.

Life carried on as normal for them although there were a few more holidays and fancy dinners. Aunt Bella spent more time with her art and started a little community theater group. Uncle Nige stayed on as a doorman. Every summer I would attend coding and AP Math classes, and then I took the class that changed my life: cryptography. No matter what I had to endure during the year with my mother and her string of losers, knowing that I would get to go to Boston and immerse myself in learning and analytics made it all worthwhile. Aunt Bella would insist on a week for us where we would visit Greece or Italy or some exotic place where I would be fascinated by symbols, and she would indulge in the beauty of ancient ruins. Uncle Nige's idea of quality time was dragging the two of us to the wonders of 'the good ole USA'.

"So, what are we talking about?"

Detective Miller. I didn't know why he rubbed me the wrong way. His sunny disposition didn't fool me for a minute. I knew this tactic well: pretend you're on their side until they trust you enough to spill their guts. Unfortunately for him, there was nothing to spill.

"Aren't you supposed to stay in your assigned seat for the duration of the flight, Detective?"

"Ally cat!" The tone was Uncle Nige's way of chastising me when he felt I was being rude.

"Oh, Ally cat! Seems appropriate. Can I call you that?" Miller said.

I had to concede he was handsome in a rugged way. And his smile had a certain come-hither quality to it, but I wasn't biting!

"Nope."

He feigned heartache and clutched his chest. "Oh, the pain. The rejection."

Uncle Nige was barely holding it together. I could feel him shaking in the seat next to me.

"He's not funny," I said, giving Uncle Nige my best unimpressed look.

"Come on, honey. Give the guy a chance."

I always deferred to him, but this time I wasn't budging. It took Uncle Nige one look at my face to know that he wasn't going to win this one.

"Sorry, buddy. I tried. I've seen that look before, and you're on your own."

"I'm sure if you get to know me you wouldn't be so tough on me." He batted his eyes, and I quickly suppressed a smile.

"Or find out that this little butter-won't-melt-in-my-mouth routine is just a ruse to figure out if I'm involved in whatever's going on with Olivia or get me into bed."

Uncle Nige groaned loudly enough to remind me that he was still within earshot and didn't want to hear that part of the conversation. He was like my dad in that way. He nearly gave himself a stroke when I was 17 and Aunt Bella tried to talk to him about putting me on some sort of birth control. He looked hurt, and I couldn't tell if it was genuine or just part of the act. Either way, I wasn't playing along anymore.

Five hours later we landed at Seattle-Tacoma airport. Most times people pray that everything goes smoothly, and they aren't delayed too long at the airport, but I didn't feel that way that day. I wanted something to go wrong so that I could avoid Riverview as long as possible. I hoped for some sort of a delay, no reservation, or even a shortage of rental cars, but no such luck,

An hour later the Welcome to Riverview sign beckoned us into the town. For the first time, it seemed real. I don't know why, but I turned in my seat and stared at the sign on the other side of the road. I hadn't seen it since Max drove me to Seattle and I had borrowed his uncle's gun to shoot it up. It was still riddled with the bullet holes I'd put there before I left. In the space next to *You are now leaving,* I'd spelled out HELL! in bullets. They'd never bothered to repair it.

Max Bennett

I checked into the Red River Inn late on Tuesday afternoon, it is just a few miles from where I grew up. The owner, Mrs. Lowe, had run the inn for over forty years. She kept to herself and didn't peddle gossip. If she knew who I was, she didn't let on. She didn't look a day older than when I last saw her. My memories of those last days came flooding back to me like it was yesterday.

It was a week after graduation. I had my diploma in hand and a suitcase with a few belongings. I had been running, blood covering my hands and face: not mine. She'd seen me crying and cowering in the back of the inn near the lake that horrible day. She's the one who called Max to take me to Seattle. She took my suitcase and ushered me into the inn, locking the doors behind us.

"You're in no state to go anywhere, honey."

She went to one of the closets and took out a few towels and clothing someone had probably left behind. Then she returned and took out a nightgown. It was the most beautiful thing I'd ever seen—soft and smelling of tea roses.

"I can't, Mrs. Lowe. I need to get the 1.30 bus and get to Boston." She looked at me with the kindest smile.

"Yes, you do. But first, you need to stop running. Take a nice long bath. Soak..." Her eyes filled with tears, but she stopped herself.

"Soak all the pain and bruises away. I'll make you a lovely meal. Tomorrow, when you get on that bus, you'll leave this town knowing that you left for something better. No one chased you away."

I was too tired to fight, so I went upstairs, keys in hand, and entered the most beautiful room I'd ever seen in my life. A canopied bed with baby blue cotton sheets and the most beautiful wing-backed chairs. It was like something out of an Anne of Green Gables novel. I couldn't stop myself from touching everything in there from the linen to the fine oak and I even sat in front of the mirror and brushed my hair for a while.

For a few minutes, I forgot about what happened. I went into the bathroom and marveled at the gold and white bath. It was shaped like a little dingy but deeper. I learned later that it was a ball and claw bathtub. It was beautiful. I filled it halfway with warm water and then topped it up with some more hot water, and after a few minutes, I understood what she'd meant. The water wound its way around my bruises and scrapes, and after the burning sensation came to relief. A hundred tiny fingers doing God's work. I found some shampoo and applied a little to my hair. It smelled of strawberry and lavender. I massaged it into my scalp, and instead of using the hand-held shower to rinse it off, I submersed my body in the warm water. Holding my breath and letting everything that happened that day just float out of the top of my head and the soles of my feet. It was a habit I'd gotten into as a child. I loved large bodies of water. Cleansing. I didn't have many occasions to bathe, mostly shower, but every chance I got, I would jump off the rocks a mile out of town and just stay underwater for as long as I could hold my breath.

I wanted to ask her if she remembered me and thank her for saving me that day. I struggled to find the courage.

"So, you came back, Alex?"

I stared at her in disbelief. "Mrs. Lowe. You remember me?"

"Hard not to, honey. I was waiting for you to say something, but I thought the better of it, and then I remembered what a meddlesome old lady I am and decided what the hell." She laughed, and I couldn't help but feel relieved.

"I'm so glad you made it out of here. Your stepdad was a right son-of-a-bitch!"

"Did I ever thank you? For helping me hide from him."

"Of course you did, honey! To be honest, seeing you today would have been thanks enough even if you hadn't."

She lowered her head and handed me the key. "This is the room you stayed in last time-remember?"

"Yes. Have you changed it at all?" I silently prayed that she hadn't.

"I'm afraid I have, but I'm sure you'll love it. We have other guests; they'll share the communal bathroom. She gave me a sly smile.

"It's nearly supper, and it just so happens that I made my famous pot roast, scalloped potatoes, and freshly baked rolls."

"Count me in." I couldn't wait to get into my room.

"Do you know where I could find a desk and a pinboard? Oh, I'm so sorry, I didn't even ask if it would be ok to set up a little workstation in the room?"

"It's your room as long as you're here, honey. Do what you like except mess up my decor." That giggle again. It was like sunshine shimmering on a lake.

"I'm sure you can find what you need in the basement, but for the board, you may have to go to Vales' down the road. They have anything artsy. The town has really changed since you were last here. Very cosmopolitan." She seemed ambivalent about it. "It's great for business but really bad for character."

"Mrs. Lowe?"

She turned around clearly eager to get back to her roast.

"When you said earlier that my stepdad WAS a real son-of-a-bitch? What did you mean?"

Her face fell, and she beckoned me to the dining room just off the corridor.

"Haven't you spoken to your mom since you left?"

Her face was a mix of confusion and dread. She seemed to be wrestling with whether or not to tell me or send me to speak to my mother.

"He took off years ago or disappeared. It was about four years or so after you left town."

I was aware of her watching me intently. Looking for some sign of relief or sorrow or joy.

"It's ok to be happy that he's gone. To be honest, most of the people in the town were. Well except Owen Long. He ran up a tab that rivaled the national debt. Owen was convinced he skipped out on him to avoid paying up."

"Did the police look for him?"

"For a while, yes, but they had very little to go on. It was suspicious, according to the sheriff."

"What do you mean?"

"Well, he apparently didn't take anything. Not a change of clothes, nothing. He had been huffing and puffing all over town that he had hit it big. Was coming into some money. Believe me, he needed it. He owed a lot of people, from the grocers to Owen and even the Parkers." She shook her head. I could almost see a shiver go down her spine.

"The Parkers, as in illegal gambling and underground fight clubs?"

"Yes, and that's just the half of it from what I hear." She got up and straightened her apron.

"Now, if you'll excuse me, my child. I have to tend to that roast, and you need to get settled."

I grabbed my backpack from the little reception desk and made my way up the stairs. I know the way to the room by heart. I let myself in and spend the next hour putting a couple of T-shirts and jeans and my workout gear away and then running a bath. Nothing like a shower or bath after a long trip.

Mrs. Lowe had changed the room, but it seemed even more warm and inviting. A light drizzle started to fall outside, and I went onto the little balcony to enjoy it while the water filled the tub. The sun was slowly inching its way over the edge of the horizon. The sky and the lake suddenly turned the color of a grapefruit. Mrs. Lowe once told me that she called it Red River Inn because it was what captivated her when she first came to view the property. I could see why. I was like watching God run brushstrokes across the sky. The more the sun set, the more vivid it became.

I drew myself away for a minute to close the faucets and then watched the master artist at work. In the middle of that blissful moment, my stepdad forced his way into my thoughts. During all those years of abuse and torment, jumping out of windows and once even a moving car, I had never been able to figure out why the man hated me so much. It was in every look, every word, and every punch and slap. The irony was that I never hated him: instead, I hated my mom. He treated her like a queen, and yet she never once tried to stop him or intervene. I could never make sense of it.

A thought entered my mind, but a knock at the door pushed it right out. It was Uncle Nige.

"Hey, Ally cat!"

"Uncle Nige, I appreciate you coming back here I know you didn't have to?"

He looked perplexed. "We've had this conversation in Boston. I'm here to look out for you. I took the room down the hall."

I welcomed him in, and he was as impressed with the room as I was.

"So, what's the plan?" he asked.

"No plan. I'm going to get settled. Go to Vale's before supper, and then have a good night's rest."

"Sounds like a plan. I'll see you at supper." He turned to leave.

"Uncle Nige?"

He stopped at the door. "Yes, angel?"

"Did you know he disappeared?"

"Who?" His brows furrowed and he closed the door again.

"John. My stepdad."

"What? When?"

"About four years after I left town. Mrs. Lowe told me."

"I didn't, but I can't say that I'm surprised or that I'm going to cry myself to sleep about it." I knew he wasn't kidding.

"You said disappeared, not killed or in jail?"

"No, she said disappeared. He was talking about coming into some money but disappeared without even taking any belongings. Isn't that strange?"

"Yes, but if he was telling the truth then maybe there was nothing worth taking."

He moved towards me and hugged me before whispering in my ear. "That part of your life is over, my child. You're safe from him now."

He left and closed the door gently behind him. Even though I didn't need to, I still moved towards the door to lock it behind him. Old habits and all.

A sudden knock at the door startled me, but I figured it was either Mrs. Lowe or Uncle Nige.

"Max Bennett."

"Hey, Harper. I heard you were back in town." He walked into the room unbidden and took a seat in one of the re-upholstered wing-back chairs.

"How did you know I was back? Never mind. You'll probably spin some outlandish yarn, and I have a bath to get to. So, what's up?"

"I'm disappointed. Not even a drink for your old partner in crime. I caught a lot of heat for letting you use my dad's gun to shoot up the sign and driving you to Seattle, and I don't even get a thank you?"

He gave me that crooked grin that used to make all the girls melt. If there was a poster child for the town's bad boy, Max Bennett was it.

"I did thank you. Just not the way you wanted." I said.

He sat back, and it was clear he was not leaving anytime soon. Luckily the bath water is still hot so I can indulge him for a few minutes.

"So, Max, are you going to tell me why you snuck in here, or am I going to have to guess?"

I offered him a beer and poured myself two Vodkas from the minibar. Despite coming from one of the wealthiest criminal families in the state, Max just wanted to be like everyone else. Dressed down, beers and burgers.

"Thanks. You remember." He seemed pleased by that.

"I figured when you left, you erased everything about this town from your mind. Me included."

Something flashed across his face, but not long enough for me to figure it out.

"You were the only thing that made this town bearable and fun, Max. I never forgot you. I just needed to get out. You know what my life was like." His face fell for a minute.

"Hey! None of that. I'm ok. You're ok. Everything turned out fine and as soon as we find Olivia, we can all go back to our lives."

He took a swig of his beer and then started to peel the label off. I remembered that from when we were teens in the woods. It usually meant nothing was ok.

"Shit. What's wrong, Max?"

"I'm not ok, Alex. I don't think any of us are."

Twisted Ties

I gulped the double Vodka in one fluid motion. Max just looked at me and then did the same with the beer. Unfortunately for him, beer doesn't work like that, and he only managed to get a third of it down before he had to come up for air.

"What do you mean none of us are ok?"

We both jumped at the sound of the rap at the door. Max reached for his gun.

"You have a gun?" I whispered.

"I told you something's going on, and now you've been lured back to Riverview."

There was another knock at the door.

"Alex. Open up, it's Adrian." Max didn't take his hand off his gun.

"Relax, it's the detective who told me about Olivia's disappearance. I trust him." He rolled his eyes.

"Ok. Do you trust him? I won't trust him or anyone, and that way all our bases are covered."

"So, you don't even trust me?"

"Seriously, Alex? Now?" I moved to the door before Detective Miller knocked again and alerted the whole inn.

He came in, and I could see by the look on his face that he knew Max. Surprised to see him here but weary too.

"Bennett. Why am I not surprised? Where there's trouble you're never far behind," the detective quipped.

"Further ahead than you, Miller. Still chasing your tail?" Max countered.

"Could you guys save the hair-pulling until you're in your own homes? Now, what are you both doing here?" I spoke. They looked at each other, and neither wanted to be the first to spill.

"Ok, then you can both go and let me get on with my life." I walked towards the door, and Miller was the first to break.

"All right, I came to check in on you and try to convince you, again, to go back to Boston," said Miller. "Someone went through a lot of trouble to get you to come back. That's never a great sign.

"I don't usually agree with the police, but I think he's right. Someone's gone to a lot of trouble to get you back here. Whatever's going on here, I think you're at the center of it."

"Me? That's ridiculous."

"Is it?" He ran his hands through his hair. "Since Olivia's disappearance, someone's taken a shot at me, tried to run me off the road, and cut the brake line on my car."

"Isn't that par for the course in your line of work?"

I didn't mean to be catty, but I was tired of people trying to tell me what to do. I didn't know what was going on, but I was not going to run. I was done being the little mouse that gets played with before being devoured by some unknown predator. I noticed for the first time that Max looked crestfallen, and I realized that he was genuinely concerned.

"I'm sorry, Maximillian."

He gave me a shy smile, and I knew that all was forgiven.

"Look, I know that you're concerned about me." I looked at Max, and he held my gaze.

"But I'm not going anywhere. That's it. Whoever it is who wanted me back in Riverview, for whatever reason, got what they wanted."

I turned to face Detective Miller. "Look, you and I don't know each other, and I don't know what your deal is or the history between the two of you. Frankly, I don't care. So, here's the deal. You both are going to leave now, and we'll meet here for dinner at 8 and take it from there." I looked at them both.

"Deal."

"Deal."

They grudgingly agreed, but they knew there was no negotiation. Not with me, at least. They left the room like chastised children, but I remembered something.

"Detective Miller."

Both men turned with a 'what now' look on their faces.

"Yes." Dt. Miller said almost sounding almost painful.

He looks uncomfortable and I stifle the urge to laugh. Miller is clearly not used to being given instructions.

"Is it possible to get copies of the report and whatever else you have on Olivia's disappearance?"

Before he answered, it occurred to me to push my luck. "And on my stepdad?"

Both men looked at me as if I'd lost my mind. I didn't know why I wanted to see his file, perhaps to make sure he'd gone or out of some misguided sense of closure.

"I can't remove the originals. Both are still open investigations. I have copies that I can bring this evening." He seemed defeated somehow.

Once they'd left, I locked the door and tested it twice, and just in case, I closed the patio door and made sure it was locked too. I went into the bathroom and locked the door behind me. I tested the water, and sure enough, it was tepid. I let about half of it out and started to top it up with warm water.

Mrs. Lowe had a wonderful selection of bath products arranged on the windowsill, and I poured a generous amount of it into the water. The lukewarm water gradually heating up was mind-blowing. Like jumping out of an ice bath and into a hot tub. The Vodka and the aroma of the bath products cast a spell on me that was unrivaled. I stayed in the water until my fingers and toes were wrinkled. When the water started to cool, I decided against adding more water and used the warm fluffy towels to dry off. I stepped in the shower to rinse off and wash and condition my hair. I wrapped myself in a clean towel and put my hair in a turban before returning to the room. Thankfully there was a hairdryer in the room, and I did a quick once-over before applying a leave-in moisturizer. Time to get to Vales, and set up the workstation, leaving just enough time for dinner.

When I arrived, I didn't pay attention to how much Riverview had changed. Detective Miller dropped me and Uncle Nige off and headed back to the station, I presumed, and for some reason, I just needed to get to the inn. I felt exposed outside.

Now that I had settled in and began to take in how different the town was since I'd been a child, it didn't seem as frightening as it did back then. I was surprised by the craft coffee shops and gourmet stores it was like walking down a cobbled street in France or Italy. It didn't take me long to find Vales. It was packed, filled with parents buying stationery and artists arguing over the type of canvas they needed for their art. The assistants barely gave me a passing glance.

This was the presence of the entitled elite, and a woman dressed like a college student wasn't worth their time. I found the pinboard and a desk that needed assembling. It wasn't heavy, but it was cumbersome, and I still needed pins, markers, tape, and a map of the town. Well, two.

"May I help you?"

A young man, no more than 14 maybe 15, stood behind me. He was new and hadn't yet figured out who the big-ticket customers were, or he had avoided them like the plague. "I'm Aaron."

"Thank you, Aaron. Could you take these to the register for me? I need to get a few more things."

He seemed so happy just to help that I could only imagine what he'd been subject to by the customers he'd tried to help before me. He was stronger than he looked and was back in a flash. I liked this kid.

"What else can I help you with, Miss?"

"Just for calling me Miss you're getting a tip." His mid-voice-breaking laugh was adorable. "I'm not quite sure, but I know that I need a couple of notebooks, sketchpads, markers, drawing pins..."

"Are you an artist? Because I am." He looked proud. "I work here so that I can get a discount on supplies otherwise, I couldn't afford it." His honesty was refreshing.

"Aaron! Get back to the storeroom. We're running low on brushes." The voice startled both of us. It was a guy in his 20s probably trying to cheat Aaron out of a commission. Aaron started shaking and turned to leave upset.

"Aaron. Come back here." I turned to face the guy.

"Who are you?" I asked.

"My name's Nick. Nick Vale. My father owns this store." His chest puffed up like a rooster pursuing a hen.

"Well, Nick Vale. Aaron was helping me so if you would just go about your business and leave us to it that would be awesome."

He looked taken aback but left us alone.

"Ok, Aaron. You were saying that you're an artist. What kind of art?"

"Mostly portraits. I want to be a police sketch artist one day. Hand and AI. I'm going to invent the first artificial intelligence program capable of creating true-to-life sketches based on people's instructions."

"That's amazing but here's a tip: don't tell anyone until it's done. People steal great ideas. And always, always register it at the patent office."

"Wow. You're really smart. How do you know all that?"

"I have a few patents, and I learned the hard way not to trust everyone with your dreams." My face must have changed, and the kid picked it up.

"You're sad."

"No, just thinking about lessons learned." I shrugged it off and gave him the rest of the list. He returned quickly with everything that I could think of.

"What's wrong?" I looked at him and smiled. "You're astute, that's good."

"Thanks, but what does that mean?"

"Well, it means you're clever and can read people and situations quickly. It's a great quality. It will take you far in life."

"I hope so." A sadness crossed his face, but I didn't want to pry. "So, what's wrong?"

"Well, I know what I want to do, but I've never done it before, and I'm not sure if I have everything I need." My mind started scrambling for anything that I might have missed.

"Ok. So, start with what you want to end up with and work backward. That's what my mom used to say."

"She sounds like a smart woman." His face fell, and his eyes filled with tears.

"She was. Then she took off."

"I'm so sorry, Aaron." I reached out to rub his shoulder, but he pulled away. "Sorry."

"Don't be. I'm just tired of being the boy whose mom took off."

"Well, you're not that to me." I thought for a minute. "Hey, are you happy working here?"

"No." He said it in a matter-of-fact tone.

"I'm only going to be in town a little while, but I could use someone to show me around and help me out." His face lit up like he'd won a place at art school.

"Let's say ten bucks an hour. Weekly and you have to keep count."

The hug caught me off guard, but I hugged him back. "Thank you. Thank you, Ms."

"First instruction: call me Alex." He looked uncomfortable, so I didn't push it. "Now let's see how good you are at the working backward thing?"

"Ok." He looked nervous but determined.

"I'm trying to figure out what happened to a friend of mine. I need to have a place to keep information. A place for speculation. Facts and maps of the town. Two maps, one of the town now an older map of what it used to look like when I left about 11 years ago."

"What about a laptop and a printer?"

"Because sometimes there are things online that you won't find anywhere else. For instance, we have a map of the town before and a map of the new gentrified town. The tourist hub." This kid was good.

"Printer yes, laptop, I don't leave home without it," I said with a smirk.

Two hours later I was back at the inn. Aaron tagged along to help me set everything up. I left him to it and went downstairs to ask Mrs. Lowe if I could add four extra people for supper. She practically levitated with joy.

"Now I have an excuse to make my peppermint tart."

"Have you seen Uncle Nige, Mrs. Lowe? "

"I think he's in his room. He went out for a walk and came back in quite a huff."

"What happened?"

"Not everyone is happy about the 'improvements' to the town." She air quoted 'improvements.'

I went back upstairs to check on him, but I changed my mind. If there was one thing Aunt Bella drilled into me, it was to let fuming men be.

Entangled

Aaron was still hard at work when it was time for supper.

"Isn't your dad going to worry about you being out this late?" He just looked away.

"Not really. I'm in foster care. My dad couldn't take care of me after my mom left."

"Well, I'm worried about you. So, get in there and wash up, mister. Mrs. Lowe is lovely, but she's a beast if you let her roast overcook." He did as he was told and was done and ready in a few minutes.

He looked worried.

"What's up?"

"I've never had a dinner at a table in a fancy place. What if I make a mess?"

"Then you make a mess. It's not the end of the world. Besides, it's not that fancy. Just watch me. OK?"

"OK!"

I ducked into the bathroom, slipped into Aunt Bella's favorite emerald and gold dress and heels, and tied my black hair into a bun. I'd never been much of a make-up and styled-hair girl. Looking back, I thought it was to piss my beauty queen mom off. It was Olivia and then Aunt Bella who taught me how much fun it could be to get all dolled up. A few strands of hair broke free, but they framed my face, so I left them alone. A few light touches of make-up and I was good to go.

I tell Aaron to go ahead. The stairway to the dining room seemed longer as I navigate my way down. I was focused on not falling because I rarely wear heels and being the entertainment for the night by tripping over my own feet was not something I was interested in. I reached the bottom and scanned the room until I saw the guys seated near the fireplace.

Detective Miller and Max were staring at me in a way they never had before, and it made my body shiver. Uncle Nige just smiled. He'd seen me dressed up before, but I thought it was the reminder of Aunt Bella that was the reason for the smile. He and Aaron were getting on like a house on fire within a few minutes. They both loved model trains, fishing it's a real bro fest between the two of them.

"Could the two of you stop staring at me as if I'm tonight's special?" Detective Miller blushed at being caught out but Max didn't even try to hide his reaction.

"No way, Harper." He started to laugh. "We're going to talk about this!"

"Nope. We're not. We're going to have a nice dinner and dessert and then we're going up to my room to brainstorm."

I looked at Detective Miller. He was staring at his starter of clams in white wine sauce so hard you'd think he was trying to find a clue.

"Did you bring the copies of the files, Detective?"

He didn't even look up. "Yes. I did."

He removed a cardboard folder from under the table and handed it to me. "Oh, and please call me Adrian."

"And you can call me Alex. Well, as long as you can look me in the eye."

He lifted his head and smiled. "Sorry, I was, uhm... just thinking about something that I need to remember to check up on."

"Anything important? I mean related to the case?"

I was all business but did manage to notice Uncle Nige and Aaron shaking their heads out of the corner of my eye. Before I could probe further, Mrs. Lowe came over to ask how everything was. After reveling in our praises, she scurried off to the kitchen and returned a few minutes later with plates piled with roast beef, sauce, scalloped potatoes, tender steamed broccoli, and roasted butternut medallions. Good old-fashioned home cooking. Nothing like it.

Aaron practically licked his plate clean, and I asked if he'd like another helping. As if sensing the boy's worry about having seconds, we all decided that a second helping wouldn't be wasted. I'd never seen someone enjoy a plate of food that much and my heart ached a little. Partly from my memories and mostly from his present. It didn't take a scientist to figure out what his life must be like.

By the time dessert arrived, I was so stuffed that I felt like I was going to burst. It was homemade peach preserve and ice cream. When dinner was done, Aaron excused himself and went back up to the room to finish up setting the workspace. The rest of us had a nightcap before going upstairs and pondering the disappearance of Olivia. No one said it, but it was obvious that we didn't know what to do next because none of us knew where it would take us. Eventually, we couldn't stall any longer, and we made our way upstairs. I cradled the case file under my arm and opened the door to my room. I was amazed by what Aaron had managed to do. Even Adrian was impressed.

"Geez, kid. You've got a bright future as a cop or FBI agent ahead of you. Can you come down to the station sometime and do this to our situation room?" Aaron beamed from ear to ear.

How he managed to move the armoire and the vanity is anybody's guess. He placed the vanity close to the bathroom door and the armoire next to the patio door, thereby creating an entire mini office that can accommodate the desk complete with laptop and printer all set up. The pinboards are placed one above the other without damaging Mrs. Lowe's walls, thank God, and the third one is positioned above the desk. The pins, markers, and other stationery are all neatly arranged on the desk within easy reach. The only thing left to do is to get to work.

"Ok. So, what now?" Max, as usual, was the first to pipe up.

"First, someone needs to take Aaron home. It's way too late for him to walk or be out." His face fell.

"Please, please don't send me home Alex." His plea broke my heart.

"Your foster mom will be beside herself with worry. I can't."

"No, she won't. Call her if you don't believe me. " Something about the way he said it made me believe him.

"Adrian. Will you call her, please? Official police business like?"

"Ok. What's the number, kid?"

Aaron's face lit up.

He gave Adrian the number, and something about his face made me think he'd made this call before. He stepped out of the room to speak to her.

When he returned, his face was ashen. I took him aside and asked what was going on. His eyes became glassy, and he said we'd talk about it later, but for now, the kid was in their care.

"Your foster mom says it's ok. Alex can look after you while she's here."

He was keeping something back, and it concerned me. Not the taking care of Aaron part, but Adrian's demeanor. Something about that call and Aaron's foster mom rattled him.

Once everything was settled and Adrian had taken everything out of the file, we got to work setting up the first board. Everything that was known about Olivia and her last movements. Everything leading up to her disappearance. She was last seen at the gala at the Riverview Country Club. According to witnesses, she'd had only water to drink and left at around 9.30 in her red Porsche.

"9.30?" Something about the time was bothering me. "Are you sure?"

"I wasn't there, Alex. That's what the eyewitnesses reported. The valet remembers giving her the keys to her car because she threw a fit about it smelling like BO. He checked the time, praying that his shift would end soon." Adrian raised his hands. "His words, not mine."

"Did you take his statement?"

"No one of the officers did. I interviewed him later at the station when all hell broke loose, and the commissioner ripped the department a new one for not taking it seriously."

I had a thought.

"Is the officer's name on the statement?" He checked the second page and nodded.

"O'Callahan."

"Could you call him?"

"It's after 10." He looks at me as if I was crazy, but then he relented and started dialing.

"Hey Berta. Is O'Callahan on duty? Great. Could you patch me through to him?" He suddenly remembered that he had no idea why he was calling. He lifted his free hand and mouthed, "What now?"

"O'Callahan. Detective Miller. I have a few questions about the night you took the witness statements at the Sinclair disappearance. Just a minute."

"Ask him if the valet who gave her the keys was the same one who parked her car when she arrived. If it wasn't him who did, but if he was, ask the officer if the valet smelled of BO?"

He questioned the officer and then asked him to hold on.

"He says he brought the car, and the guy mentioned that it smelled of BO, but the officer didn't notice a smell from the guy."

He figured out what I was getting to, and suddenly, the wheels in his brain whirred to life.

"I need you to track down the valet and find out who was there to park the car when Olivia arrived."

He listened for a few minutes and then barked at the guy.

"I don't care if you're off in thirty minutes. It never dawned on you to find out if someone had access to the victim's car, and now, we have an heiress missing and a valet who could have skipped town by now. Just find out who was on duty when she arrived, and I'll do the rest."

He went to sit in the wingback chair and pulled his hair back. "Shit." Everyone was silent. "I can't believe I missed it. It's so obvious."

"We don't know anything yet. Let's not jump ahead. In the meantime, can we look at the time again?"

Max walked over to me and stood a little too close. Adrian leaped out of the chair, and pretty soon, I was wedged between them.

"Guys, can I get some room, please?" They both slunk back. I turned to Adrian.

"Remember back in Boston, when were we listening to the voicemails?"

"Yeah. What about it?"

I walked over to my bag and removed the phone. I typed in the numbers to access the voicemail and put it on speaker. Olivia's eerie message came on again once I hit saved messages. After listening to each voice message, I hit either save or delete.

Adrian and everyone else looked at me in confusion.

"Listen to the time the message was left." I replay the message. Date and time. 11.45 pm. Suddenly, they got it.

"Wait a minute. So, she left you the message over two hours after leaving the gala?" Max and Adrian exchanged looks.

"That's right. And that's not all. Listen." I played the message for them again. "Can you hear that? That weird metallic sound?"

Aaron piped up. "That's the hallway at my school. She'd using something to make the lockers rattle."

"How do you know that son?" Uncle Nige asked him.

"I get bullied a lot."

He looked down at his feet and started swinging them. I started to suspect that he was younger than 15 and just little for his age.

"That's the sound the bullies like to make. It's like they saw it in a horror movie."

I looked at Adrian and Max and then at Uncle Nige. We didn't know whether to deal with Aaron being bullied, which none of us were equipped for, or to check out the school. Eventually, Uncle Nige took the bullet.

"You guys go and check out the school. I'll stay here with my new buddy. We'll have some hot chocolate and smores and watch old movies." The smile on Aaron's face said he loved that idea and made me feel better.

"Did the police ever check out the school?" I asked Adrian.

"We never had any reason to. I don't think it ever even came up in the investigation."

Both Max and Adrian checked their guns before we left.

"Is it just me, or does this get weirder by the minute? I mean, what in the hell is a rich girl doing in a high school two hours after she's disappeared? Making calls to a friend she hasn't seen in nearly ten years?"

"Eight years!" I corrected him.

"We're headed to Freddy Krueger's stomping grounds, and that's what's bugging you?"

Personal Stakes

Knowing that Aaron was safe with Uncle Nige helped me concentrate on the task ahead. Max drove while Adrian pouted in the back. It didn't help that Max and I chatted away about old times, which left Adrian with nothing to contribute. I tried drawing him into the conversation, but Max would keep bringing it back to our history.

"How come I don't remember you from school, Adrian?" Max shrugged. He was always prone to tantrums when he wasn't the center of attention. Some things never change.

"I didn't attend school in Riverview."

"Really?"

"I went to Bryce Academy in Devland Falls."

He didn't say it in a proud or bragging way. That struck me as strange because Bryce Academy was a private school in the state. Most of the wealthy families in Riverview sent their kids there, and competition was fierce. Cutthroat fierce.

"That's impressive. I didn't realize you were a Bryce Boy." He snorted.

"I'm not. Scholarship kid and the other children reminded me about it every day." He went quiet, and I knew it was the end of that topic.

"Olivia went to Bryce. Until she was expelled. She never would say why." I don't know why that memory suddenly popped into my head, but it seemed on topic, so I let it go.

"I know. It was the talk of the school. She was flunking English and threatened to accuse the teacher of sexual assault if he didn't pass her. He refused. She made good on her threat, and he killed himself. By the time they found out that she was lying, her parents had already whisked her away to a school in Switzerland until the heat died down. Then brought her here to Riverview High."

"Whoa... Dude! Don't you think that's information that would be useful for us to know?" I was livid. Why would he sit on information like that?

Adrian kept quiet for a while.

"It was gossip. You know what children are like. Especially entitled brats. They had nothing going on in their lives. When Olivia was expelled, there was every kind of story you can think of doing the rounds. It didn't help that Mr. Olsen died at the same time."

"It's still a lot to sit on, Adrian. Olivia's missing, and we have nothing to go on. It may be nothing, but that wasn't your call to make."

I didn't know if I was angry at him or angry that all this time, everyone had been assuming that this had something to do with me: when maybe it had nothing to do with me at all.

"Look, Alex. I'm sorry. I should have mentioned it, but I didn't want to muddy the waters by dredging up history. I just wanted to find this girl, and once you throw too many scenarios or leads into the mix, everything goes to shit."

I got the sense that he wasn't talking about Oliva's case anymore.

Max took his phone out of his jacket pocket and punched in a number by heart.

"Vin. Max. Listen, I need you to smooth the way for us. Riverview High. We'll be there in ten minutes. Can you handle it? " He ended the call.

"What was that?" Adrian and I asked simultaneously.

"That was me arranging for us to get into the school with tripping alarms, getting caught on camera, or otherwise ending up in jail for misdemeanor breaking." He gave me a sideways glance.

"You used to be a lot cooler!" The statement landed like a knife.

"Yeah, well it's easy to be cool and not give a damn when you have nothing to lose." I folded my arms like a petulant child. "That was a cheap shot, by the way."

"Just telling it like it is."

I let out a snort.

"What's that?"

"It's called a snort of derision. A.K.A as the sound someone makes when someone is full of shit!"

"I'm full of shit?"

"Yep."

"Please enlighten me, Your Highness. How am I full of shit?" He was huffing now. Got him. I knew exactly which buttons to push.

"No thanks. I don't have that kind of time. Besides, we're here."

"I'm not letting you out until you tell me what exactly that means."

"Max. Do you remember what happened when you refused to let me out of that headlock in third grade?" His hands reflexively covered his crotch.

"You wouldn't?"

"Wouldn't I?" I looked him dead in the eye and didn't blink. He unlocked the door.

Even though the area surrounding the school was clear, Max at least had the presence of mind to park in the dark canopy of trees just outside the school. I remembered it well. The kids would ditch class and come here to make out, fight, smoke joints, and even just hide. I spent a lot of time here. I used to dream about buying a plot of land and building a little cabin on the lake. Live alone and write or something else that doesn't require interacting with people.

We made our way to the front door of the school.

"What are you two doing?" Max said in a stage whisper.

"Can't you see the massive lock on the front door?" He pointed toward it.

We followed Max around the back and waited while he scanned the perimeter. He spotted the opening that his friend must have arranged for him. He ran across the open AstroTurf grass to the open door. A couple of good yanks and we were in.

"Are you sure that this guy can be trusted?"

Max didn't answer me. Tantrum.

"Don't worry about it, Alex." Adrian took the lead. "If anything happens, I'll just pull rank and say that we were driving by and saw something suspicious."

It was pitch dark, but I reached for his hand and gave it a grateful squeeze.

"If you two are done playing handsy, can we do what we came here to do?"

"What is wrong with you? You've been like a bull with a blocked nut since we drove over here." Suddenly a sound silenced us.

"It's probably the security guard." A few moments later, the beam of a flashlight confirmed it. His walkie-talkie crackled to life and called him to the other end of the campus.

"Thank you, Vin!" Max breathed a sigh of relief.

"How do you know it was him?"

"Have you ever heard of a security guard being called to an emergency at a high school?"

I hadn't, but I wasn't about to admit it. Not when he was being such a pill.

"Come on the lockers are down here." I walked ahead, but Adrian grabbed hold of me.

"I think you should stay between Max and me. Max can walk in front, and I can cover the flank."

I didn't argue because, well, they both have guns, and it makes sense.

"You do remember where the lockers are, right, Max?"

"Very funny. Max didn't come to school much."

He gave me a wry look and then inched ahead.

"It's such a putdown coming from the class valedictorian!"

Ouch. That was always the one thing Max and I could do well. Fight. He was the one guy in my entire life who never let me get away with anything. He gave as good as he got. If I'm honest, I loved it.

We turned left after the cafeteria and came face to face with half a mile of lockers.

"Damn!" I let out an involuntary curse.

"What?" Adrian had been so quiet I forgot he was there.

"There are three floors of lockers."

"Shit. I forgot about that. How in the hell are we going to figure out which rows? Then we have to figure out what she was trying to tell you?" Max doubled over like he'd had the wind knocked out of him.

Adrian scanned the hallway trying to figure out how to tackle this conundrum. "What if we call in the cavalry?"

"What?" Cavalry?

"You mean the cops? Are you insane? How are we going to explain what we're doing here? That a 13-year-old led us here based on a voicemail?" Max was freaking out, but he made a good point. There was no rational way to spin this.

"Wait. Aaron said that he recognized the sound from being bullied," I said.

"Yes. So?" Max let out an exasperated sigh.

"Think about it. It's summer vacation. He just turned 14, which means he was in eighth grade when he was bullied. Where are the middle school lockers?" I try to convince him.

Max started running to the third floor. Eighth grade was the last time he showed any interest in school. He graduated with a B average in his senior year, and it still baffled me how he did it without attending school... well, regularly. He attended enough to avoid being disqualified for not meeting the minimum attendance, but that was Max for you.

We eventually caught up to him, and it didn't take us long to find the locker I was meant to find. A postcard stuck out of it. The words *Friends Forever are* spray painted on the door, and bloody fingerprints are on the lock.

"Don't touch it, Alex," Adrian's voice instructed me, but he sounded so far away. I couldn't move. A glimmer of gold caught my eye:

a necklace, carefully threaded through the vents on the locker. It was half of a heart with a picture in it: mine.

The Traitor Within

The police were there in 15 minutes. Every officer whether they be on duty or off was sent. The school was a hive of protective-gear-wearing forensic technicians. I watched as they set about doing their work. Detective Miller was at the center of the fray, reviewing every bit of evidence after it was bagged. He was working his ass off. I was to remain where I was to be questioned, but unfortunately for them, I don't take orders well.

I left to get coffee from the local coffee shop. I only became aware of a car tailing me as I approached the entrance. I wasn't afraid because it was Max doing what he always did when we were kids. He pulled up near the entrance and rolled down the window just as I was about to go inside.

"You have no sense of danger do you, Harper? I've been driving behind you for a block and a half," he said with a sly grin. Same old Max.

"I thought you were still obsessed with... what did you call it? Checking out my ass as I walked!"

He laughs. "Yeah, well, there's that too."

"Still haven't caught up with the whole women's rights thing, huh?"

His face turned serious. "Yes, I have, Harper. I'm not the guy you remember." He looked deadly serious.

"OK, so you're not still involved with a lot of shady people and... what's a good way to put this, 'criminal entrepreneurship?' "

He grinned and shrugged. This was how he used to infuriate me when were younger. Max Bennett could never answer a straight question.

"You know I hate it when you do that. What do you think? That I'm going to snitch to the police?" I turned and entered the coffee shop. Surprisingly, considering the time, it was full. Another mercy was that no one was at the counter. Max sidled up to me while I waited to be served.

"Sorry, Harpy!" I elbowed him in the shoulder. "Sorry, I know you hate that nickname. Just trying to break the ice."

"Yes, I do, and what ice?" I' was confused. "We were literally together an hour ago. Until the police were on their way when you ran out of there like a rat out of a burning meth lab." He started laughing. It was the kind of laugh that made other people laugh.

The barista came to take my order. I noticed from his name tag that he was also the on-duty manager, which was good.

"Evening. My name is Gabe. What can I get for you today?"

"Well, Gabe, I've got a big order and I need to know if you and your staff can handle it and also deliver it to the high school and repeat the order in another two hours. I'm willing to pay upfront."

"We can certainly do that, no problem. Is this for officers there?"

"Yeah!"

"Can I suggest something?" He didn't wait for me to answer. "We have a pop-up truck/trailer thing that we could come and set up outside. We use it for festivals etc. It's fully equipped."

"Awesome. That would be great, Gabe. Thank you. Could you add pastries, too? Which kinds?"

"They're cops, so I'm thinking everything you've got that won't be needed here. They'll be there and ready to go by the time you're back at the school."

He wanted to ask me something but lost his nerve. I let him. It was probably about the case, and I had no ideas to offer.

"Before you ring it up, could you add one large latte with three shots of espresso?"

I turned to Max and asked if he'd like anything. He just stared at me blankly.

"You're buying coffee and snacks for all the cops there?"

I was not in the mood for this. I was tired, shaken, and cranky. I turned back to Gabe.

"Make that two. We'll wait for them."

Gabe was at the top of his game. Within 10 minutes, we were on our way back to the school. Well, I was. Max, skipped it, obviously.

Gabe was right. By the time I arrived, they'd already set up. I went and asked for another triple-shot espresso latte for Detective Miller. I stopped to put on the disposable booties and headed inside. I told the officers outside to get some coffee and nearly caused a stampede. As I walked through, I yelled about the free coffee and pastries outside. I ended up having to do it on every floor until the third. I handed Detective Miller his coffee and told the remaining officers about the pop-up. Everyone made their way down except the five tech people who couldn't.

"Can you ask one of your guys to bring five coffees up for the tech people?" Miller called a junior officer back, and he went and asked them.

Pretty soon it was just me, Detective Miller, and the techs. He came to sit next to me on the cold concrete step, clearly happy for the break and probably the coffee. He took a swig.

"Thank you for this. It's kind of you."

"Pleasure, Detective."

He looked at me, a shy smile lighting up his face. "I think you can call me Adrian."

"OK." I turned serious for a moment and took a long, slow sip of the coffee, and my life was just better for a few moments before the inevitable fall to earth. "So, have they found anything besides the stuff in my old locker."

"Zilch. The problem is the school was cleaned just after summer break began. We're trying to get hold of the janitor. Can't reach him. Sent two officers to his home, and nothing."

"Are you trying to find out if it was cleaned regularly?"

"Yes."

"I can help you with that. No, it wasn't."

He looked at me with a mix of distrust and awe. "How could you possibly know that?"

"My mother's husband used to be the janitor here when we were in school. It gets a thorough once over after it closes and then another just before school starts."

"Why do you say your mother's husband and not stepdad?"

"We're not there yet, and I'm not the case you're investigating."

He grabbed the back of his neck. "I'm sorry, that was stepping over the line."

"No, it wasn't. Get over yourself. You're a detective trained to pick up on the smallest inconsistency. I get it. It's just in the past."

He knew when to shut it down and turned to walk away.

"Hey, Adrian, something's not right."

"What do you mean?"

I sniffed the air and then got down on the floor and sniffed again. "Is the janitor's closet still in the basement?"

I ran down the stairs to find the room locked. "Shit"

"What's going on? Why do you need to get in there so badly?"

"I can't explain until I get in there."

"Well, that helps." He wasn't even bothering to disguise the sarcasm.

"OK. Have it your way." Before he knew what was happening, I picked up a nearby wrench and broke the lock open.

"What the hell did you just do?"

"Haven't you been paying attention? Trying to get into the janitors' office." I went in and immediately started going through the cleaning products. My heart started racing.

Adrian reluctantly followed me in.

"Notice anything odd?

"No, but then I'm still in the dark about why we're even here."

I ignored him because sometimes my mind moved too fast, and I didn't have the patience to explain, it frustrated people, I know. But sometimes trying to explain my process turned the clear thought muddy, and it went away.

"The cleaning solutions are pretty standard. The mops are new. Never been used."

"You're thinking someone cleaned up, and instead of washing the mops, they just replaced them." He shook his head.

"OK, then you explain why a section of the third floor smells like a mix of ammonia and turpentine while the rest of the floors don't. Look around: no ammonia or bleach."

"You think someone used the two to clean up?"

"Schools aren't allowed to use ammonia or bleach because of the harmful side effects, especially for kids with conditions like asthma or accidental ingestion. Someone tried to clean something up and needed something that they hoped would leave no trace."

I ran back upstairs and waited for him to catch up. I took his hand and told him to close his eyes. As were walking, I told him to block everything out and just smell. He opened his eyes and looked at me, astonished.

He called one of the techs over and asked if they'd used luminol to detect any blood in the area.

"We're moving quadrant by quadrant. We haven't made it here yet." The guy looked worried, as though he was going to be yelled at.

"OK, could a couple of your guys take a few minutes, come over here, and do it?"

"Sure."

He left and returned with another forensics guy.

This one picked up on it immediately. "I'm getting the distinct smell of ammonia and bleach... maybe. That's going to cause a problem. It interferes with the efficacy of luminol and makes it impossible to pull DNA."

"Let's just try anyway."

Adrian's manner of speaking to them was unlike that of any cop I'd ever dealt with. He made people want to help him. The guys got to work spraying the luminol, and Adrian found the main light switch for the floor and plunged us into darkness. The area they'd sprayed lit up like a Christmas tree.

"Jesus," they all said in unison.

It was on the walls above the locker, the ceiling boards, and the floor.

While the techs moved their attention to where the blood had been found, I could tell they were not happy about it. There was no way to link it to Olivia or anyone else. Whoever did this knew what they were doing. I sat on the steps and watched them while absentmindedly kicking at a loose linoleum tile.

"Adrian, do you have a knife?"

"No, why?"

"Just a hunch... please could you just trust me?" He relented and asked the assembled techs and cops if anyone had a knife.

"We have a scalpel." One of the crime techs volunteered and handed it to me.

"Thanks." I got onto the floor and started working to lift the tile. No easy task.

One of the senior officers yelled at Adrian.

"Why are you letting a civilian tamper with a crime scene? This is not how we do things, Miller!"

"Oh, shut up, Bukowski. You've been sitting with your thumb up your ass for months, and it took Alex a couple of days to get us this far."

I was focused on what I was doing, but his defense of me didn't go unnoticed. Finally, I managed to pry the tile loose, and just as I expected, there was blood underneath. The officers went silent. The tech guys were excited because this might mean that there were viable samples in places the ammonia and bleach couldn't reach. Pretty soon they were in a frenzy of evidence collection.

I'd done my part, so I decided to go get some rest. As I was heading out, Adrian came after me. We were just a few feet from the blood and surrounded by officers.

"Hey... uhm... Look, I'm sorry for being such a dick back there." He looked me dead in the eye, and I knew he was being sincere.

"It's cool. Don't sweat it. I've dealt with policemen before. It's not the first time I've had to jump through hoops. That is what you were doing, wasn't it? Sizing me up?"

"Yes."

"Good!"

He looked at me in disbelief. "Good?" He seemed confused that I wasn't angry or upset.

"If you took everything and everyone at face value, you'd be a crap detective."

He laughed. "You're something else, Alex."

"You don't know the half of it!"

"Would you like to get coffee sometime or a bite to eat?"

"Sure..." Suddenly Adrian faded into the background as my eye caught the pattern of the panels on the ceiling. My ADD and OCD, I knew, could be both a blessing and a curse.

"What is it? What's wrong?

"The ceiling. It's disorganized. Some of the panels are faded while others look brand new." I knew I needed to get up there and fix it, or it would drive me nuts.

"I'm sorry. It's a big ask, but until I fix it, I'm not going to be able to rest."

"It's OK. Let me see if I can find a ladder."

He disappeared and returned a few minutes later, ladder in tow. By then I'd figured out that it was my OCD that was causing the anxiety. This was the exact spot when Olivia and I were young and fearless. We would move a panel, use the lockers as a makeshift step stool, and sneak out and go smoke on the roof. Sometimes we even went sunbathing, when the weather permitted, and we resented being forced to sit in a classroom.

Adrian returned with a ladder from the basement.

"Will you hold it steady for me, please?

"Of course." I paused a moment. "Let me borrow your gloves."

He dug a fresh pair out of his jacket pocket and handed them to me.

"Wow. A real-life boy scout."

He smiled. "You joke, but I was."

I got to work on the panels, placing them in order. But some of them wouldn't budge when I tried to lift them.

"Do you have a flashlight? "

"What kinda question is that to ask a cop?" He handed it to me. "What do you need it for?"

"Something's weighing a few of the panels down, and I need to climb up and see."

That plan seems like a waste of time because we'd have to move the ladder for me to gain proper access. I handed the flashlight back to him.

"This won't work. I'm just going to try to move them until they pop out instead of trying to push them up."

It didn't take me long to figure out how thanks to my OCD, which caused difficulty with some people but helped me make connections in seemingly random events. I felt the panel give way and in a matter of seconds I was knocked off the ladder by the heavy object that had been holding it down. Everything just stopped, and I wondered who was screaming before I realized it was me. Screaming at the cold, dead eyes, staring at me, of the body hanging upside down like a kid on a playground structure.

Deadly Confrontations

I sat in the back of an ambulance being attended to by paramedics for the usual post-trauma conditions. "Did you hit your head? Did you pass out?" The more I insisted that there was nothing wrong with me, the more questions they asked. I knew they were just doing their jobs, but all it did was aggravate me.

Adrian came out to check on me. It had only been 10 minutes since I discovered the body, but it seemed longer.

"How's the patient doing?" he asked one of the paramedics, who side-eyed me before answering.

"Physically, she's just a little bruised. Nothing broken or torn. But man, could her personality use a tune-up."

"Hey!" My gaze bored holes into him. "There's nothing wrong with my hearing."

He slunk off.

"Man, you have a real way with people. Our town's own Miss Congeniality."

He meant it as a joke, but before I knew what was happening, I was sobbing. Like most men, he didn't know what to do at first. Crying is kryptonite for most men, but to my surprise, he climbed into the back of the ambulance and held me. Just held me. No questions, no trying to fix it or probing. It felt good being held like that. I pulled myself together.

"I'm sorry. I don't know what came over me."

He didn't pretend to know or offer solutions. He just sat there.

"Have they taken down the body yet?"

"No, they need to be careful. It's practically skin and bones. They have to be careful. Then some poor bastard will have to climb in there and do an evidence sweep. Looks like we're going to be here all night."

Suddenly a loud crash came from the school, and we both took off to find out what happened. When we got to the third floor, all there was was dust and broken panels. The techs were scrambling to make sure that they collected everything. One of the officers came up to Adrian.

"We don't know what happened, Detective. One minute they were taking pictures and samples and the next thing it all just came down."

He looked around to call one of the tech guys over, eager to not be blamed, but Adrian nixed it.

"Leave them to finish." He exhaled deeply. "We can figure all that out later. It was probably just structural, too much strain from the way the body was hanging half out of the ceiling."

"Can I have your flashlight again, please?" Before Adrian could retrieve it, the officer had already taken his out of the holster on the side of his uniform.

"There you go, miss."

Adrian gave him a look, and the guy walked away. The hole in the ceiling was by no means small, and it was still pitch black up there, but something caught my eye. I turned the light on and cast the beam over the still intact portion, trying to find what it was that jumped out at me. A woman's heel. She lay dead still.

"There's someone up there," I told Adrian, who had turned to talk to one of the tech guys.

He jerked around. "Jesus Christ, not another body."

I focused on her back with the flashlight. "No. I think she is still alive."

He turned to one of the officers and told him to get the paramedics up here ASAP.

"We need them to confirm if she's alive and figure out how to get her down."

The officer ran down the stairs, and within minutes, the paramedics were on site, complete with a gurney and mobile ECG machine.

"How in the hell are we going to get her down?" one of the paramedics said out loud. "The fire department is better equipped for this."

Adrian lost it. "So, you want to sit around and wait for the fire department to come and bring her down to you and then we can figure out if she's dead or alive. Grab the ladder and get your fucking ass up there. Our first priority is to confirm if she's alive."

She just nodded her head, and one of the officers helped her with the ladder, but her partner volunteered to go up instead.

"Be careful. We don't know what condition the rest of this ceiling is in."

He didn't take his eyes off the body. I didn't know which outcome he was hoping for, but I did know that either way, Adrian Miller was right in the eye of a storm. Cases like this made careers or broke them.

"She's alive. The heart rate is dangerously low. We need to evacuate her immediately."

His partner got on the horn and requested an emergency helicopter.

"Her vitals are failing," he told Adrian. "We need to get her down immediately."

We could hear the chopper approaching, and time was of the essence. No one in the group had ever dealt with something like this, and we were all left scratching our heads.

I looked around and saw the stretcher. "Is this detachable?" I ask the female paramedic.

"Yes, it is."

"OK, we're going to take it off. Pass it up to your partner and have him secure her in it."

We jumped into action, and while the officers were trying to figure out what we were doing, the paramedic and I passed the detached stretcher up. As an afterthought, she handed him a neck brace and anything else she could think of to keep the woman from further injury.

"She's secure. Now what?" he asked.

"Every available officer, please come over here." They listened, surprisingly, considering I was not an officer.

"I need six of you to position yourself on every third step of the ladder. The rest of you make sure it's secure and please, please can those of you who are left stand behind the officers on the ladder to make sure they don't get hurt."

They got into position as instructed. The helicopter sounded close like it was landing.

I looked up at the paramedic.

"OK, now you slowly turn the gurney and slide it, don't lift it." He did it and then looked at me.

"The officers at the top grab the front as he slides the gurney out, resist the urge to lift it. Like you're guiding a child down a slide. Once you have the front, slide it to the next couple of officers."

It took about ten minutes, but we got her out and onto the stretcher. They carried the stretcher down with the help of a couple of officers, and the woman was loaded onto the helicopter and whisked off to Seattle General. The local hospital wasn't equipped for this, whatever this was.

Adrian came over to me. Before he could say anything, I interrupted.

"Shit!"

"What?"

"I didn't even look at her to see if it was Olivia."

"Dammit. Me either. I gotta go. I need to get to Seattle General."

I walked out with him. I needed my bed and a hot bath.

"Are you OK to get home?"

Seemingly out of nowhere, Max appeared. "Don't worry about it, Officer. I'll get her home safely."

Adrian gave Max the once over. These two had clearly crossed paths before.

"Are you sure?" Adrian asked again.

"Yes. I'll be fine. You just get to Seattle General."

He started up the car, but before he left, I touched his arm. "Please."

"I know. As soon as I know, you'll know." He drove off, and for some reason, I watched him leave.

Max honked the horn. "Hello! Are we leaving or what?" He was clearly agitated.

"What's eating you?"

He just huffed. "Nothing."

"You're such a bad liar. Ironic, considering your profession."

"Well, Ms. Know-it-all, it may surprise you to know that my profession, as you put it, doesn't involve sitting and waiting while you make goo-goo eyes at the good detective."

I burst out laughing. "Who even says goo-goo eyes anymore?"

"It's still a word."

"I know. OK, I'm sorry. That was inconsiderate of me." I looked out the window. "And for the record, I wasn't making eyes at Adrian. I was saying a silent prayer that it's Olivia we found and that she pulls through."

"Wait a minute, they found Olivia?"

"Well, we found a woman. We don't know who she is yet. Or how she fits into all this. Anyway, I'm getting way ahead of myself. All I know is that right now I'm tired and need to get into bed."

"Is that an invitation?"

"Seriously Max, you hear tired and bed and that's where your mind goes?"

He looked away. "Just having a little fun with you, Harper. Don't take the world so seriously. None of us are getting out of it alive!"

Something about what he said sent chills down my spine. My aunt Bella used to say it was someone walking over your grave.

"It's easy for you to say. You didn't just get knocked off a ladder by a dead body and then find another one not even an hour later."

He kept quiet for a moment and then asked, "If it is Olivia, what was she doing up there?"

"I don't know." I took a deep breath. "For that matter, what was the corpse doing there? It was clearly up there for a long time. How desperate was she to hide in a ceiling with a dead body?"

"How long do you think she was up there?"

"Probably only a few days. The paramedics said that she was severely dehydrated. How she got up there is anyone's guess."

It wasn't long before we pulled up in front of the inn. It felt like coming home.

"I'll walk you to the door."

"That's really not necessary, Max. I'll be okay."

"I know you will, but I'm doing it more for myself." He paused. "To know you're safe."

I unbuckled myself and turned to look at him. He struggled to get the words out. "I know what your life was like when we were growing up. I didn't know how to talk to you about it or even help you. I'm sorry."

"It's okay, Max." I touched his hand. "It really is. Everything turned out okay. Aside from a few personality defects and impulse control problems." We both laughed.

"Look, you need to stop carrying that around with you. There's nothing you could have done. Plenty of people knew. Child services were sent to that house so many times I knew the social workers by name."

I let myself out of the car. "Aren't you going to walk me in?"

He smiled at me and climbed out, too.

I let us in. Everyone was asleep. When we got to the door of my room, I knew something was off. I gave Max a look, and he took the key from me and went in ahead of me.

Nothing looked out of place. Everything was still where I'd left it. Maybe my mind was just overtired and hyped up, making me see ghosts around every corner.

"Damn, I'm tired. I'm even starting..." It was then that a gift-wrapped box on my pillow caught my attention.

Max followed my gaze. "Is that like those chocolates they leave on pillows in fancy hotels?"

My breathing became heavy and labored. There was something about knowing a stranger had been in my space that did this to me. I walked over to the side of the bed where the box was. It was no bigger than a jewelry box. I pulled the ribbon off and opened the lid carefully.

Max was right beside me; I could practically hear him hold his breath. It was the other half of the locket from the school, the one with Olivia's picture in it. The only difference was that the picture was recent, not the original one of us as teenagers. I sank to the floor. This was just too much.

Max took control and called the police. They arrived within a few minutes. By then, Uncle Nige, Aaron, and Mrs. Lowe were up and milling around me, trying to comfort me. I was feeling overwhelmed and wanted to be alone, but when Det. Bukowski walked in, I was glad they were there because this guy seriously pissed me off. Thankfully, Max dealt with him, and he behaved himself.

He didn't spend a long time. He was in and out in less than 30 minutes. Ass!

After he left with the other half of the locket, the gift box, and the ribbon, Max and the others insisted on staying a little while. Mrs. Lowe made me a large pot of Chamomile tea. She wanted to cook, but I insisted that I wasn't hungry. I couldn't keep anything down anyway.

Eventually, Uncle Nige left, but Aaron insisted on staying on the reclining chair. "It's cool. I've slept in worse places." It broke my heart because I knew it was the truth. Mrs. Lowe said good night and gave me the best hug.

"I'm so sorry about this, Mrs. Lowe. I'll find another place to stay first thing tomorrow."

"Why? Have I done something wrong?"

"No, it's me. I'm like a curse. I can't put any of you in danger anymore." Her face changed, and she got deadly serious with me, angry even.

"Now you listen to me! You're not responsible for any of this, Alex. You didn't put us in danger. There's someone out there hurting people, and he seems to know that you can stop him. So do that and stop taking responsibility for other people's messes."

"Yeah, yeah." Uncle Nige chimed in.

I started getting emotional but reined it in. I'd cry in the shower. I even began to feel guilty for feeling sorry for myself when I thought of how much worse Aaron had it.

"Mrs. Lowe, do you perhaps know how long Aaron's been in the foster care system?"

"Foster care? No, child, he's not in foster care. His mom left for work one night and never came back. That was about a month ago." She shook her head.

"Personally, I don't buy it. I think she suffered the same fate as Olivia. The things that happen in this town since all these wealthy people have moved in will make your hair stand on end." She paused for a while.

"Anyway, she left him with a neighbor, and for the first week, it was fine because she'd send money. When the money stopped that's when Edna, his caregiver, stopped playing nice. Making him find work or he doesn't eat and sleeps in the chicken coop most nights. She won't even let the poor kid wash up properly in the shower. Has to clean himself outside."

My heart broke for him at that moment. I knew something was amiss, but I could never have imagined the extent of it.

"Why didn't anyone call the authorities?"

She looks at me with a hurt expression on her face.

"Why would you assume that we didn't?"

She stopped talking. It was the most awkward pause I'd ever been part of.

"Every time we'd call, they'd send someone out, but nothing got done about it. All they ever say is that his mother left him in that horrible woman's care, and they see no reason to remove him. Plus, he never speaks up for himself."

"I'm sorry for the assumption, Mrs. Lowe. It was out of line. My heart just breaks for him. He's such an amazing kid."

I stopped talking because a thought just popped into my head, demanding answers. "You said his mother left for work 'that night'?"

"Honey, let's you and I go and sit in the kitchen."

I asked Uncle Nige to come along because this sounded serious.

I checked on Aaron. He was out cold. We closed the door and checked the latches of the windows just to be safe. Then, we made our way to the kitchen. Both Uncle Nige and I pulled up a chair and sat at a quaint little antique table. Mrs. Lowe started on the hot chocolate. Eventually, she brought the mugs over on a tray and sat down. She took a long sip after blowing on it for a while.

I wasn't the most patient person, but I did know when to push and when to let people build the courage to do difficult things or talk about difficult topics.

"You remember what this town was like. A real community. Yes, there were bad things, and people were battling to get by. When the new money people moved in, and the area was transformed, it was a good thing for everyone. We thought. But with wealth and opulence comes a certain way of thinking and that includes people as commodities and a belief that they're above the law. Even though it really got bad with the influx of tech millionaires and billionaires it was always the with the old money set. Ask Nigel?"

Nigel looked at her, and she regretted her error instantly.

"I'm sorry, Nigel. I thought you'd already told her."

"Told me what?" I looked at both of them, but Uncle Nige was the first one to break the silence.

"My family are part of the old money group. I grew up with that decadent lifestyle but some of the amoral things I just couldn't live with."

"So, that's why you left?"

He looked away. No, it was something far worse than that.

He drank some hot chocolate and asked Mrs. Lowe for some whisky for courage. She brought a bottle and put it down. He opened it up and poured some into the hot chocolate. I'd never known Uncle Nige to be so afraid. It was making me afraid. He was my rock. The only constant in my life. I didn't think I could bear it.

"My parents used to hold these parties. Their friends would come to the house and all these young women from Riverview and the surrounding towns would be there and basically get bid on."

He stopped to see my reaction, but all he found was a blank stare.

"I never took part in it. I was in love with Bella and wanted to make a life together. She thought I didn't want to introduce her to my family because I was ashamed of being in love with a girl from the wrong side of the tracks, but..."

"You were trying to protect her from them?" He nodded, tears streaming down his face.

"One night, at another one of their parties, I saw Bella. I tried to convince her to leave, but she was hurt. She thought I was ashamed, and I couldn't make her see reason. She was fiery and stubborn. You get that from her. I went back up to my room to get my car keys, but when I got back down, she was gone. I searched the estate and every room in the house for her. We didn't know it then, but she was carrying our child.

"You have a child?"

"Yes. We have a child. When I found her, she was sitting in the gazebo and sobbing. She'd found out what kind of party it was in the most horrific way possible. She wouldn't say what happened—or rather who happened—to her." He took another sip. "She only told me years later. When we were in Boston."

"What happened to the child?" He began to squirm.

"I insisted on at least taking her to the police station, and it was during the exam that she discovered she was pregnant. With you."

He looked up at me, trembling with fear. I could see that he was concerned with my reaction. I had none. I had just shut down.

"I'm so sorry. We should have told you, brought you to live with us, all of it. She thought it would be better for you to grow up here in Riverview. She thought you'd be safer with her sister. She wanted to start a life in Boston."

"And I would have held her back? Is that it?"

"No, Alex. No. She didn't know how she would manage both. She was still healing from what happened to her. She really thought it was the best thing for you. We had no idea what kind of life we were condemning you to."

"And still you left me. Sent me back here every time the summer was over."

I got up from the table and went to my room and sleep. I took a couple of tablets out of my bag and washed them down with some vodka from the minibar. It hadn't sunk in for me yet, but I could hear Uncle Nige wailing downstairs. My last thought before I drifted off to sleep was, "I really never had anyone. Not even Uncle Nige and Aunt Bella."

Point of no return

I didn't know how long I'd slept, but when I got up, my body felt uncoordinated, even wobbly. I was still groggy from the sleeping tablets, but I needed a dreamless sleep. I didn't want to think or analyze for once; I just wanted my brain to shut down and leave me in peace. I'd have killed for some coffee but couldn't face going downstairs just yet. I got in the shower and got dressed. Hopefully, I could sneak away to the coffee shop for a few hours and get my mind together.

So much of what I heard answered unasked questions but also brought back a profound sense of rejection. That was what I was struggling with the most: the people who made me feel the most loved in the world were also the ones who gave me away to be raised by a monster.

Aaron was already gone. He'd left a note saying thank you and that he'd be back later. I didn't like the idea of him out on the streets alone. Understandable, given the fact that he needed to work to eat. I really hoped he came back.

There was a knock at the door.

"Ally cat? Are you up?" It was the first time in my life that I didn't want to see or talk to him. I knew he had a slew of reasons and thousands of apologies, but I couldn't deal with any of that right now.

He left, and I could hear him going down the staircase and out the front door. I figured that it was safe to sneak out. Thankfully, no one crossed paths with me, and I walked the few blocks to the coffee shop.

There was a new barista on duty. I ordered a dirty chai with two shots of espresso and something to eat. I was starving. As I waited for my order, I sat at a table with a clear view of the school. The police had long since left, and a crew had been brought in to clean up and repair the damage. Somehow the slow and methodical way they went about it centered me.

Adrian came into the coffee shop.

"Can I join you? Of course, you do look like you'd rather be alone."

"You're an empath now? "

"A what?"

"Empath. Someone who can sense feelings or tap into other people's pain."

"Nope. Just a guy grabbing something to eat and taking a chance that a beautiful woman will allow me to join her."

"Sure. In fact, I'm glad you're here."

"Really?"

"You seem surprised."

"Well, to be honest, I wasn't sure that you'd want to spend time with me."

"Why?"

"Well, with your recent legal troubles and me being a cop?"

"Hey, you're right. I forgot about all that. You can go, I've changed my mind!" We both started laughing, and a waiter came over to take Adrian's order. He ordered a BLT and black coffee.

"Would you like us to bring your meal now or would you want it brought at the same time?"

"Same time, please? But you can bring my drink now if that's okay."

"Mine too, please."

We sat in comfortable silence for a while. It was nice.

"So do you wanna talk shop or anything else?"

"Shop. Definitely. I'm not ready to veer off on another tangent."

"Is the woman okay?"

"Nope, she still hasn't regained consciousness. Looks like she was drugged, assaulted, and left for dead."

"Is it..."

"Olivia? No." He paused as the waiter brought our drinks. "We're still trying to identify her and her connection to this. Unfortunately, we can't do anything until she regains consciousness."

"We can try to identify her. Work backwards from there."

"And how do you propose we do that?"

"Let's just say I have skills."

He smiled. "I bet you do."

If I wasn't mistaken, Detective Miller was flirting with me.

The waiter saved the day when he brought the food. I liked him, but I was dealing with too much. It wouldn't have been fair to bring him into all this drama.

"What do the doctors say about her condition?"

His face suddenly turned dark. "It's not looking good. Something horrible happened to this woman, Alex."

"Did you know that Aaron's mom also disappeared a few weeks ago?"

"No. I didn't. Around the same time as Olivia?"

"Either that or a few days apart. What I'm wondering is why all the effort for Olivia, all police resources and TV coverage, but nothing for that little boy's mom."

He took a bite of his toast, retrieved his phone from his pocket, and hit speed dial.

"Bukowski, can you put together all the missing persons reports filed in the last two months for me? I'll pick them up in 10." He hung up.

"I don't know how you work with that guy. He's such a prick."

"No argument here."

"Even last night, when someone left the other half of the locket on my bed, he was barely there for thirty minutes. Didn't even ask me for a statement."

I saw the look on Adrian's face change.

"Alex, what locket?"

"When I got home last night, someone had left a gift-wrapped box on my bed. It had the other half of the locket in it."

"That lousy SOB. I saw him last night and this morning, and he didn't say a word." He was fuming.

"Why would he do that?"

"Looking for promotion and wants to take point on this case. He's been undermining me at every turn. It's like campaigning."

"Because it's a high-profile case."

"Don't know. But what I do know is I need to track down that locket."

He got up to leave. "I'm sorry I have to leave you here alone, again." He dropped a twenty on the table and headed off to the police station.

I continued eating my breakfast and forced last night's revelations out of my mind. I remembered that I forgot to ask Adrian about the other body and called him. He picked up almost immediately.

"What's wrong?"

"Nothing. I just need to know if the other body has been identified yet?"

"No. We've had to send it to the FBI to assist. The was nothing but bone for us to work with."

"You wouldn't be able to send me a picture, would you?

"I'm not supposed to, but I will."

"Great, email it to me. I have an idea. The woman in the hospital too."

"Sure, but I don't know how much you'll be able to do with either. Her face was so badly smashed in that it was completely distorted. But hey, your wish is my command, as they say."

I finished up and headed back to the inn to get to work. My kind of detective work.

I got home, and Mrs. Lowe, Aaron, and Uncle Nige were sitting around the table, having breakfast. I greeted them, and Aaron jumped out of his seat to hug me. He insisted on coming with me upstairs. Even though I told him I needed to work, he wouldn't budge.

"You can come up after you finish breakfast, how's that?"

I turned to go to my room but called him back.

"If I ask you a question, will you promise to give me an honest answer? I won't get mad, I promise."

He was scared and started quivering.

"It's okay, kiddo. No need to be scared, I promise."

He relaxed a bit but was still anxious.

"How old are you? Really?" He hesitated for a moment. "Thirteen and a half."

"Okay. Where's your dad?"

He shrugged. "It's always been only me and mom. Anytime I ask she'd say he died."

"You didn't believe her?"

"Not really, but she's my mom. The night she left, she said she was going to him to get what we deserved."

"So, she was going to meet him?"

"No, not exactly. She was dressed for a party, and she said she'd found out he was going to be there."

"Okay. I'm sorry for all the questions. You can go finish your food."

"It's okay. No one ever asks me anything."

I entered the room and turned on my laptop. Adrian had already sent the pics. The victim, the skull of the remains we found, and the skeleton.

I was going to have to work fast to avoid detection. Hacking into sophisticated systems, especially government ones, was illegal and tricky. I needed access to the imaging program that I designed and sold to them a few years ago. Luckily, I'd installed a trojan horse that could allow me access to it without being detected.

I uploaded the skull first and the woman's face. And now for the part that the FBI never had any interest in, so I never shared it. The program could be instructed to put a face on a skull using virtual depth and tissue markers, and it could also reduce and approximate what someone may have looked like before their face was damaged or bloated from being in the water for a long time.

While I waited for that to be rendered, I started a deep dive on the web looking for missing young women in or around Riverview. Then, as an afterthought, I searched the society pages for any parties or events that took place the week Aaron's mom disappeared.

Nothing came up about Aaron's mom's disappearance only Oliva's. The lifestyle section proved more promising. There were two parties: one at the Linderbrooks' Estate and another at the Sinclair's home. There were literally hundreds of photos to go through.

The program had finished both renderings. I saved and downloaded both, and then got the hell off the FBI server. I knew that there was no way that they could detect me, but I could do without the hassle. I'd spent enough time with them. In fact, the reason I was a person of interest a few months ago was that I'd designed and sold them a few programs.

I printed the pictures out. I left them at the printer while I mentally prepared myself for the tedious task of going through two online lifestyle galleries with easily 300 pics each on them. I made some instant coffee using the in-room kettle and supplies.

When I was sure I was ready, I'd just made myself comfortable at the table when there was a knock at the door. Thinking it was Aaron, I got up and opened the door for him. Instead, I found Max and Adrian at the door. Aaron pushed through their legs and went to turn on the TV.

I didn't ask them in because I was up to no good. Max would be impressed, but Adrian would definitely have major issues and so many questions. I didn't notice Aaron get in until he asked for a soda from the minibar. I just yelled 'Sure' over my shoulder and turned my attention back to the two men.

"What's up, guys?"

"Well, I came to check on you. See if I could help. He's probably here to arrest or interrogate you. Who knows with these officers?" Max just couldn't stop himself from taking digs at Adrian.

"Actually, I came to update you. I just don't think I can in front of a guy with known criminal associations." Max laughed and prepared to launch into another attack.

"Alright, Alright! Time out, you two. Look, I don't know what this back and forth between you is about, but it stops now. There's a problem in this town and it looks like it's only the three of us willing to do something about it. So, from now on no name calling, jibes, cheap shots. Got it? Or get out!"

They looked at each other. Getting out wasn't an option for either of them.

"Alex?" Aaron called from behind me.

"Yes, kiddo?"

He started whimpering.

I turned around and saw that he had one of the printouts in his hand.

"Why do you have a picture of my mom?"

"What?" I took the printout from him and stared at it. Max and Adrian had come to stand with us.

"This is your mom?"

He nodded and started crying. I handed the picture to Adrian and started trying to console him.

"Detective Miller here rescued her last night. She's in the hospital.
"

"Is she going to be okay?"

"Honey, I honestly don't know, but the doctors are doing everything they can to help her."

"Can I go see her, please? "

I looked at Adrian, and he looked at me. I didn't want him to see her like that, but if the worst happened and she didn't pull through, he'd spend his life resentful of being kept away from her. I wasn't a mom, but I knew one. I left the room and went and asked Mrs. Lowe for help. She scrambled up the stairs. I'd already filled her in on Aaron's mom's condition, so she knew what she was in for.

We walked back into the room. Max and Adrian were chatting away while going through the gallery of Sinclair's party. I had to push down my irritation.

Mrs. Lowe took Aaron into the bedroom to prepare him for what he was about to see at the hospital. She didn't believe in protecting children from the truth: only that you could prepare them and teach them how to handle it.

"So, do you still want to go?" He didn't miss a beat.

"Yes. She's my mom."

"Let me get my things, and I'll take him."

"You've got important things to take care of here." She turned to Aaron.

I bent down to his height and took his face in my hands.

"Are you sure you're okay with me not coming along?"

"Yes. But you have to promise to be here when I get back."

It was a promise I didn't know that I wasn't going to be able to keep.

Dark Secrets

Max, Adrian, and I spent hours pouring over both galleries. Nothing unusual jumped out at us. We didn't even recognize most of the people.

There was a knock at the door, and Max popped up to open it. It was Uncle Nige. He's waving a white flag: well, it was a serviette on a chopstick, but he was trying to make amends. I wasn't there yet, but I told him that it was okay to come in. Besides he might know some of these people.

"We're drawing a blank on these pictures," I told him as he pulled up another chair.

"May I?" he said to Adrian, who was operating the laptop.

He went back to the first picture in the Sinclair gallery, about two hundred pictures ago. We all groaned, but he ignored us. He clicked on the first picture to enlarge it and then studied it intently.

"I can't believe they still do this kind of thing."

Adrian was confused.

"This isn't a party, son. It's a livestock auction. Poor naive young girls lured by promises of money, fame, even love, and they fall for it every time."

"What are you looking for?"

"I'll know when I see it. You have to remember I haven't seen most of these people in over 25 years."

"Okay, you see these two men? They're Olivia's uncles. Scumbags both of them. As we go through the pictures look out for the young girls who look out of place, nervous, awkward, and then identify the men and women they're standing close to."

Max and Adrian looked at him with confusion. I couldn't explain it myself, so I just didn't bother.

"It means that they've 'bought' the girls for the night or just for the party."

"Oh, God!" Max exclaimed, then buried his head in his hands. "I'm such a fucking idiot."

Everyone's attention was on him now. I could see he was on the verge of tears. Max Bennett never cried.

"I know these girls. My uncle Frank would call and ask me to do him a favor." He started pacing.

"He had these friends who needed a ride to a party, and he couldn't take them. I drove these girls to whatever horrible thing happened to them that night. And the weird part is I've never seen any of them again."

We all kept quiet because frankly, we didn't know what to say.

"Listen, Max," I said. "You're going to have to deal with that later, but for now we need to go through all the pictures and identify the guests and the girls."

To their credit, the guys helped me work nonstop over the next few hours to identify as many people as possible. Considering that there were close to seven hundred pics in both galleries, that was not an easy feat.

They'd identified most of the guests, and some—but not all—of the girls. They also managed to find Aaron's mom and Oliva in about a dozen of the pics. Those are the ones they started poring over because although the girls were captured, the man they were with was just out of the frame. Just his tuxedo and hands were visible. Uncle Nige enlarged the pictures slowly and let out a loud "Fuck!"

"It's cool. We all are a bit frustrated." Max's attempt at consolation totally misread the room.

"I'm not frustrated. I know whose arm that is: my father."

"Wait, he bid on Olivia Sinclair that night?" Adrian was perplexed. "How can you tell from a simple pair of cuff links?"

"He had three sets designed for me, my brother, and himself. They're completely unique. See the pattern in the inlay? It's the family crest with his initials at the bottom in diamonds. BBP III—Brian Bailey Patterson the third."

While Adrian was furiously jotting down notes in his police-issue notebook, Max kept trying to identify the other girls. Uncle Nige stopped Max on another picture: it was one of Aaron's mom. In the next picture, she was talking to someone, again with no face, just a right shoulder. Uncle Nige enlarged the picture until he could identify the almost identical cufflinks as his father's.

"Let me guess, your brother?" Adrian was in full investigator mode.

"How can you tell the difference? It could be the same man."

"No. You see that barely visible nick on the edge of the cufflink?"

"Yeah."

"Well, I put it there the night I tried to kill him."

"You tried to kill him?" I couldn't believe that this man who I'd known my whole life was capable of attempted murder.

"I would have succeeded too if the security guards hadn't intervened."

"When was this?"

He looked at me, his eyes red, and then looked at his shoes. "The day after your mother told me what they did to her."

I excused myself and went to sit in the coolest place I could find: the bathroom. I started sobbing, really sobbing, thinking of what they'd had to endure. All I could think of was my childhood. All that pain and she still loved me. They loved me.

I was in the fetal position for an hour until I was all cried out. After that came the rage. I got up off the floor and splashed my face with some cold water. I went to rejoin them. Their concern was clear, but they also knew by now that the sobbing was all I'd needed. No further discussion was necessary.

"What's the plan, guys?"

Adrian's phone rang, and he didn't look pleased with whatever he was being told. He hung up.

"Bukowski calling. Says there are no missing person's records for girls in the last few months, and as a bonus, the FBI somehow lost our remains and the other half of the locket."

"Do you buy it?" Max looked at him from his seat at the table.

"Why would he lie? I know he's angling to push me out."

"It's too convenient. You've been so focused on him muscling you out when maybe what he's doing is what he's paid to do by these rich bastards?"

Adrian just stared at Max. "You mean he's on someone's payroll to make their mistakes or problems go away?"

"Need more convincing? Look at the pictures after Aaron's mom talks to your brother. She has been forced outside, it's subtle and doesn't draw attention, but someone's definitely leading her out of the party!"

"So, whoever took her away also tried to kill her?"

"But that doesn't explain how she got into the ceiling at the school."

"Every kid who went to that school knows about the loose boards. She probably figured she'd hide up there until he left and then was too weak to climb back out."

It was true every kid—well, every kid who wanted to ditch a class or school for the day—would use those boards.

Adrian considered the theory and conceded that it had merit. I could see that he was struggling to put the pieces together in his mind and explain the loose ends.

"Whatever it is, someone is pulling the strings behind the scenes. Taking care of the messes, trafficking the girls, and getting rid of them when they become too problematic."

Uncle Nige was right. This couldn't be a one-person operation; this was a network with one puppet master orchestrating everything. But who? This had been going on for decades right under everyone's noses, and salaried police officers were making things go away.

"Wait a minute though, what about the dead body?" Adrian was trying to make the one odd piece fit.

"The body, I forgot." I went to the printer and removed the page from the tray. I froze. I couldn't stop looking at the picture. Adrian and Max both came towards me. Max took the page and stared at it in horror.

Adrian was lost. "Who is this? Would someone please tell me what's going on? What's the deal with this guy?"

Max battled to get the words out. "That's Alex's stepdad. The one who disappeared a few years ago."

"So, he's been there for how long and no one notices or smells him?" Adrian was dubious.

"Do you remember lockdown, detective? He could have been murdered and hidden up there long enough for the smell to go away."

"So, we've got the who and the what, but I'm going to need help with the why?" Adrian grabbed hold of his head and sat down.

I thought about it for a few minutes before it hit me. "Aaron!"

"Aaron?" Max turned to me. "What's he got to do with this?"

"He told me earlier that he'd never met his father, but on the night she vanished, his mother had told him she was going to go find him. She knew which party he'd be at. What if she was going there to get him to help her take care of their child? And well... the rest we can pretty much guess."

"What about your mother's husband?" Uncle Nige knew I hated him being called my stepdad. I gave him the first smile of the day since yesterday's bombshell.

"Money," I said flatly. It was the only thing he cared about.

"He was killed for money?" Adrian looked across the table at me.

"Yes, he was the janitor there and maintained some people's gardens. Rich people rarely pay attention to the help, and maybe he stumbled on some information and decided to blackmail one of the families."

"So, they killed him?" Detectives are worse than lawyers, I swear.

"Adrian, haven't you realized yet what kind of people we're dealing with?" Max answered. "Alex is right. The guy was a dick. When they expected a once-off payment, he saw an ATM, so they just got rid of him. Poor bastard was probably at the school when he was murdered, and they stashed the body, planning to come back, and then lockdown hits."

Adrian was still trying to process all of this when his phone rang. "You guys know that there's still the small matter of proof, right?"

After answering, he went silent and exhaled. Dammit, what now!? I couldn't handle any more bad news or dead bodies turning up. He hung up.

"Aaron's mom just died."

Cryptic Culmination

My heart was breaking for that little boy. I was so glad Mrs. Lowe was with him; otherwise, I'd be a wreck. He'd crept his way into my heart. I tried calling Mrs. Lowe, but it went straight to voice mail. That was weird. Maybe her battery died. That was probably it.

I didn't know if I was concerned or paranoid, but once one of those took hold, it was hard to shake.

"Adrian, who called to tell you that she died?"

"The on-call doctor. Why?"

"I'm trying to get hold of Mrs. Lowe, and she doesn't seem to be answering. Goes straight to voice mail."

"Okay, let me call the doctor back."

"Oh and ask him what happened before. Did Aaron get to see her?"

Max sidled over to me. "What's going on?"

"I don't know, maybe nothing? I just have a bad feeling."

"Ugh, you and your feelings. Since we were little."

"So, the hundred bees that stung you after you decided to streak through an open field, that feeling was nothing. Or the electrocution or trying to cross a river on a log..."

"Alright, alright..."

Adrian returned, a worried look on his face, and it made me anxious. "I just spoke to the doctor, and he says her vitals were improving, they'd drained most of the blood from the head wound, and she was even showing signs of coming out of the coma. He can't explain what happened, but then he wasn't there the whole time."

"We need to get to the hospital."

Both men agreed to take me, and an argument ensued.

"Okay. That's it, I'll call a car."

"No, no reason for that. We can compromise. We can go in my car because it's faster, and Adrian can drive because he's a cop, and if we get pulled over, he can get us out of it!"

Adrian had a cat-that-ate-the-canary smile on his face, which, in typical Max fashion, he ruined. He opened the rear passenger door for me, tossed Adrian the keys, and then proceeded to get in the back seat, too.

"Hey, I'm not a chauffeur. This is bullshit."

"Look, I'm getting tired of you two."

Adrian took a deep breath and started the car up. His anger was gone for a few moments at the roar of the engine. Then he took off like a bat out of hell. We basically flew to the hospital. The drive was typically one hour, but we were there in 30 minutes.

"What the hell were you doing?"

Adrian looked at me, suddenly ashamed. He'd obviously let his ego get the better of him.

"If you ever pull a stunt like that again..."

"I won't. I'm sorry, Alex. That guy just gets me so riled up."

"Yeah, and he's having fun doing it. Maybe if you stop letting him rile you up, he'll get bored."

I walked into Seattle General and asked which floor Sabrina Costas was on. The nurse directed us to the fifth floor, where the coroner was already overseeing the transportation of the body for an autopsy. Thankfully, the officers and coroner knew Adrian, and they let us take a look at the body.

I'd never been squeamish, but knowing that a little boy's whole had just changed forever made this pretty hard to take in. Adrian was doing his detective thing and trying to get more information out of the officers and coroner. He wasn't getting much, I could tell, because he looked more frustrated than usual.

Max was flirting with the duty nurse, and I was left in a room with a dead woman. I stood looking at her body and then the tubes and

IV needles that still needed to be removed. I went outside to call the doctor, and he came into the room with me.

"I don't know how much more I can tell you. This one's got us stumped. We really didn't think she'd make it. Just like that her vitals started improving, and there was real hope that she'd pull through." He shook his head.

"I actually wanted to ask if that was normal?" I pointed to the IV bag.

"The IV? Yes, it's how we get the medicine into the patients."

I smiled. "Yes, I know. I mean, are those droplets on the line normal?" He looked at me and then the IV. He called the nurse in to ask her who changed the IV.

"When I came on duty, I checked, and it was empty, and then I put on a new one. But I followed the procedure. I made sure there were no air pockets or damage. I swear, doctor." She was visibly upset. She was basically being accused of accidentally killing a patient.

"Nurse, can I ask? How soon after you came on duty did you change the IV?" She was fighting back tears but managing to hold it together.

"I'd say about fifteen minutes. I remember because I was just finishing when her mom and son came to see her. When she heard his voice, you could see her vitals improve. I finished up and left them alone. Well, her alone." She could see the surprise on my face.

"What do you mean you left her alone?"

"The patient's mother. She asked for a few minutes alone with her daughter. I remember the little boy was very upset. He kept saying she wasn't her mother. I just chalked it up to the stress of seeing his mom that way."

"You should have chalked it up to him telling the truth. That woman wasn't the victim's mother, and I guess that she used her time alone to either inject air or some other poison into the intravenous line." I looked out the door and called to Adrian.

"I think Mrs. Lowe killed Aaron's mother."

I spelled it out for him, and he bagged the IV and tubes for examination.

"Nurse, did the victim receive any shots today? Special medication into the IV?"

"No, she wasn't scheduled for anything until tonight."

I picked up the medical waste bin at the foot of the bed and pointed to the syringe inside.

"Is this a standard hospital-issue syringe?"

"No." The doctor looked into the wastepaper basket.

"Nurse Tuft is right. This looks like the kind of syringe a vet would use."

Adrian took it and bagged it for evidence.

"Nurse, do you recall which way they went?"

"He went into the room to see his mom because I told him visiting hours were almost over, and then he came running out of the room and disappeared. The older lady tried to find him, but she was too slow."

"Do you think he could still be in the hospital hiding?"

I wasn't sure, but something told me it was worth a shot. Aaron is a very smart kid. I turned and headed to the nurse's station. After being told repeatedly how important it was that I find him, the nurse wouldn't budge until Max came up and charmed her pants off. She relented and let me speak into the PA system for the floor.

"Aaron, honey. It's me, Alex, Max and, Adrian. If you're hiding away from the bad lady, you can come out. You're safe. We're here just outside your mommy's room. Please come out." After several attempts, I gave up. He was clearly not here. Then, just behind me, I heard the pounding of feet, and he grabbed me around my waist. It was the best feeling in the world. I turned around and hugged him so tight that I was afraid I was hurting him, but he just hugged me back.

"What do you say we go home and find another place to stay?"

"Can we just get away from here?"

"Yes, I promise."

I told the guys to go ahead and that we'd meet them in the underground parking lot. They hesitated and then went ahead.

"You know, Aaron, sometimes people mean to keep their promises, but for some reason, they can't. It happens. Do you understand?"

"Yes. It's okay to make a promise you want to keep, but sometimes you can't."

"Exactly." I ruffled his hair, and we headed out to catch up with the guys.

"Do you know where they are?"

"Yes. The green section number 3C. "

"Could you find it? "

We reached the doors to the lifts, and he pressed 3.

When we got back to the inn, I didn't waste any time packing up and getting us the hell out of there. Adrian already had the entire Riverview Police force over to comb the inn from top to bottom. I found a great-looking rental home on the lake with a pool.

Max and Adrian were over watching a game as there wasn't anything they could do on the case but wait, and I sat on the porch watching Aaron in the yard trying his best to act normal but knowing that he was wrestling with the loss of his mom and feeling helpless knowing that he should be having the carefree, loved-to-bits life every kid should have. The guys came out and joined me.

"We didn't want to leave you sitting here all by yourself."

"I told you, Max, you have the worst poker face. You can't lie, either of you! It's halftime and you guys are hungry, right?"

They nodded like naughty schoolboys.

"In the kitchen. Nachos, hot wings, tacos, chips, and beer in the fridge."

They slunk off. They came back a few minutes later with pyramids for plates and a six-pack. Max was the first to broach the subject of Aaron.

"So, what's going to happen to the kid?"

"I'm going to happen to him. I'm going to apply to be a foster parent, I know it'll be a long shot. If I get to be one then after a few years if he wants me to, I'll officially adopt him."

"Have you told him?" Max asked between mouthfuls of nachos.

"Not yet. I want to see what the courts say first. No sense getting his hopes up if they turn me down."

"Why would they turn you down?" Adrian stopped eating and looked at me.

"I have a past. Checkered history with the police and FBI, plus I'm a single girl in her twenties."

"Anyway, here comes Aaron. Drop it."

He tip-toed up the porch steps. "Can I have some nachos too, please?

"Sure but go wash up."

Adrian starts for the door, then looks back and whispers "My mom was a single mother and it was hard for her to work multiple jobs and everything she had to give up for us to have."

We were silent. It was the first real thing he'd shared with us.

Adrian's phone rang, and I could see the relief on his face even though it was work.

There was a grim look on Adrian's face as he came back.

"Oh God, what now?"

"They found Mrs. Lowe dead. Bullet to the back of the head."

I felt a mix of emotions because I genuinely liked her until she became evil incarnate.

"So, what does this mean?"

"In the criminal world, it means that our villain was just a small fish in a much bigger pond. Bullet to the head: that's straight-up execution."

Before Max could finish chewing and pick up where he'd left off, Aaron came traipsing back in looking for his lost sneakers and to cajole me into dishing up some nachos for him. They were his favorite. He could do it himself and I knew I should let him, but there was something about feeding a child. I was leaping ahead, thinking of him as my child. I had to pull back because I didn't want to imagine them saying no. When we got to the kitchen, he climbed onto a barstool and swung his legs waiting for his plate. I loaded it up and handed it to him.

"Can I watch a show?"

"Sure, but Adrian and Max are watching the football game. It's halftime now so don't say anything until I give you the sign to go watch in your room."

"Okay. Why do you guys like teasing each other so much?"

"It's what friends do."

"Really?"

"Yes, as long as you're not being mean or saying something cruel."

"Okay."

I headed back out as the sound of a show came from the TV room.

"Aw, come on, Harper! You're letting the kid watch a show on our big screen made-for-NFL-games TV."

I just laughed, and both of them frowned at me. "You've got a real sadistic streak, Harper," Max said.

"Hey, kid. Do your uncles a solid and go watch your show in your room."

"Uhm, I'll think about it."

"Hey Alex, do you have any lip balm, my lips are cracked and they hurt from the nachos," Aaron asked

"Check in my backpack, the one I brought with me from Boston." It felt like a million years ago.

Uncle Nige came home, having been up at 4 am to go fishing. "Great day on the lake today. You boys should have come with me."

"Catch anything?"

"Are you kidding? Trout, black crappie, and a largemouth bass!"

He was so excited; it warmed my heart. It was the happiest he'd been since Auntie Bella died. It still felt weird to call her mom. The person I thought was my mom was still alive and kicking. Uncle Nige even loves being a "grandpa" and dotes on Aaron.

"Wouldn't some beer-battered fish be great right now?" They tried not to make eye contact, but I'd show them.

"That would be great, guys. Uncle Nige, why don't you show the guys how you gut, cut, and fry your special batter?"

"Alright, but you don't get the secret ingredient. Well, go wash up. Let's get to it. We're wasting daylight."

I was sure they could hear my howls of laughter all the way to the bathroom.

"Alex?" I turned around. Aaron was holding my backpack towards me and scrunching his face.

"Something smells really bad in here. Like that time I found a dead cat on the side of the road."

My mind raced back nearly three months. I hadn't packed anything that could decay in my backpack. I went to the picnic table in the yard and started emptying the pack. Soon Uncle Nige and the guys were back outside and gathered around me and the pack. It contained mail and the other cellphone that I'd completely forgotten about. Oh, and the unopened parcel that turned out to be the source of the smell the minute it tumbled out.

"I think I'm going to throw up." Max was never one for blood and gore.

Adrian stepped forward and used a discarded bag from the contents of the backpack to cover his hand and a pen to hold it steady. He tore the wrapping off to reveal a jewelry box. He opened it, causing Max to keep his promise and completely redecorate my climbing ivy.

"This is bad," Adrian called for the tech team and officers to attend to the scene. When I went to see what was in the box, it was a severed finger.

Under Pressure

"This is never going to be over, is it?" I asked Adrian as we sat waiting for the reinforcements to arrive. I'd told Aaron to stay in his room. They arrived a little while later and dusted for prints, checked for clues, and put every single thing into evidence bags.

"When did the package arrive?" Bukowski glared at me.

"The day before Detective Miller came to Boston. I'm not sure. The other doorman brought it up to me."

"And the unopened mail? Are you in the habit of not checking or opening mail?" I gave him one look and decided that this ended here.

"What the hell is your problem because right now you're behaving like a whiny little dick. You know full well what hell I've been through, and you have the nerve to question whether or not I open mail."

"Calm down. I'm just doing my job."

"And which job is that exactly, the one the taxpayers pay you for or the retainer that the people on the hill pay you to make their messes go away? Get off my property. Right now. I don't care who takes over, but I am not dealing with you."

He made his exit.

"All yours, Miller. Good luck."

Even as angry as I was, I could have sworn that his 'good luck' sounded more like a threat than encouragement.

"The tech people are going to be here a while why don't we get out of their way and go get a cup of coffee in town? Your da — Uncle Nige is here."

"It's okay. You can refer to him as my dad. I kinda love it. But I'm not there just yet, you know?"

We walked back to the house, but not before Adrian told the cops that no one gets access to the evidence. As soon as they were done, it should be brought here for him to go over.

When we walked into the house, Max was ending a call and looked like he'd seen a ghost. We both stared at him.

"That was my Uncle Nico. Word on the street is that a hit is out."

"On me?" I couldn't believe it.

"On all three of us." He shook his head.

"Bukowski?" I asked Adrian.

"He's a flunky. If he is part of this. When someone orders a hit on a police officer, a woman with a young child, or one of their own, it's usually someone at the top of the food chain. "

"So, what do we do now? Lie low? "

He laughs. "Please stop watching police procedurals, I'm begging you."

"No need to beg. After all this, it's romantic comedies and stand-up. Maybe those cooking shows and the home makeovers."

"So basically, everything but police procedurals."

"Well, good luck with that, soon-to-be mom!"

"Stop it, you're going to jinx it." I was shivering, and he took his jacket off and draped it over my shoulders.

"I know the judge who was assigned to review your case. As of tomorrow, he's all yours."

"If this is a joke it's not funny, it's mean." I started sobbing my eyes out. I knew then how much I wanted this little boy in my life.

Aaron obviously heard me crying and came out to see what was wrong. He was afraid, I could tell.

"Is it about me? Is it bad? Are you sending me away?" His eyes filled with tears.

"No, no, Aaron it's all good. Don't cry. It is about you, but it's good. At least, I think it's going to be good news. I hope you will too."

"What is it?"

"Adrian just told me that he spoke to the judge, and she's going to let you stay with me for a while. And if you want to later, I can adopt you."

"What's adopt?"

"It's like when you love someone so much you want them to be part of your life forever."

"Like you'd be my new mom?"

"Yes. If you want."

He hugged me so tightly. It never dawned on me that a 13-year-old can be angst-ridden when they're not sure where they may end up.

"You already are my mom," he whispered in my ear.

They were like a song, the most beautiful words I'd ever heard. Max didn't want us to see him cry, so he was pretending to watch the techs work. Uncle Nige was blubbering.

"So how do you feel about being called grandpa?" It was then that I got there. "It's okay, Dad. I'm happy too."

"So, what do you say we go out for a beer or coffee? Mom's choice!"

"Are you crazy? Have you heard a word I've said?" "

Of course, but are we going to hide our whole lives? The person behind this wants us to go into hiding, and you know what that tells me? They're scared shitless."

I'd never seen Adrian so strong-willed. It was kind of sexy.

"You kids go. I'm going to stay here and look after my grandson. Start teaching him about bait and tackles. "

"Okay, let's go. See you later, Max." Adrian's tone was mocking.

"Just let me make a quick call."

"To whom?" I asked Max.

"To someone I'd hoped I'd never speak to again in my life. "

He hit the call button, and the person on the other end picked up. "Hey, pops, I need to talk to you."

He returned a few minutes later but didn't say a word.

"So how did it go?"

"Same. You know, the usual speech." Max put his jacket on. "So, are we going or what?

"Are you even going to tell us what the call was about?"

I was bursting with curiosity. He never talked about his family. I only knew that his dad walked out on them when he was about Aaron's age.

"I was talking to your dad this afternoon when he came back from fishing. He was carrying on about the factory farm, but in between all that, he said something that struck me, he said that sometimes to catch big fish you have to use an even bigger one. I just called in the biggest fish I know. And that's all you're getting."

We went to the coffee shop. I had their apple pie and ice cream, Adrian just had coffee, and Max... well, Max ate an entire main meal. You'd have thought he hadn't eaten all day. We had fun, and as we walked to Max's car, we were just ordinary people in a nice seemingly trouble-free town.

I asked Max if we could swing by my 'mom's' place. The ring on the finger in the box had been bothering me all day. It was unique, and I knew that I'd seen it somewhere before; I just couldn't think where.

We pulled up outside, and as expected, she came out drunk. From what I could see she had all her fingers, so I decided to leave her in peace.

The sound of screeching tires was my first clue that something was about to go horribly wrong. Both Max and Adrian jumped out. The men got out of the car and aimed at Max first. Adrian jumped in front as four shots were fired. I tried to run towards them, but my body spasmed out of control as the butt of a gun smashed against the side of my head.

My last image was of my mother screaming and running in the house.

Showdown

Current Day- Hospital

I woke up to the sound of beeping and pumping and a very, very sore head. In fact, once my headache starts, my whole body feels like it's been broken apart and stitched together wrong. A nurse comes in, and when she sees that I'm awake, she calls for the doctor.

"You are one lucky young lady." I try to speak, but he tells me not to.

"We need to remove the tube in your throat. I have to warn you, it's going to hurt. The painkillers you're on will help somewhat now, but I'm afraid it's going to take a little time for the throat to heal and not be as painful. The rest of your body, well... that's going to take weeks."

I give him the side eye. He and the nurse carefully, but not painlessly remove the tape holding the tube in place and then the tube. I'm struggling to speak, and the nurse hands me a small whiteboard and marker to write.

How long have I been here? She reads it and answers for about seven days.

"Is there anyone we can call? You had no identification on you, which made it hard for us to track next of kin."

I write down the names of everyone I know.

A few hours later my dad came in. He cries as he hugs me. My body hurts, but it's not so bad. Aaron stands in the doorway.

"What's wrong, buddy? Don't you want to give me a hug?"

He bows his head and starts crying.

"You said you'd never leave me!"

"I'm sorry, kiddo, but some very bad men took me away. I didn't leave you on purpose. I'd never do that."

He comes closer to the bed. First, he rubs my hand as if to see if I'm real and then slowly cradles himself next to me, and I don't want him to ever leave. Max comes in. His arm is in a sling but otherwise, he looks okay.

"Where's Adrian?"

The men shuffle their feet and look down. I start crying, and then in walks Detective Miller, practically in a full-body cast.

"What the hell happened to you?"

"You really don't remember? I got shot protecting this numbskull." He tilts his head towards Max but winces in pain.

"So, catch me up."

"Well, the guys who carried out the hit on us were found floating in the river a couple of days later. They'd been tortured badly, probably to get information about who they were working for."

Bukowski walks in and I can't help it. 'Fuck it' is the first words out of my mouth.

"Haven't I suffered enough?"

"Alex, Alex it's cool. Bukowski or Detective Andrew Talbert was just undercover. They knew that there was a trafficking ring and that some officers were being paid off. It's been a tough week for the department. Nearly a dozen arrests and they're naming names to get lighter sentences, avoid general population in prison." Adrian looks especially proud.

The nurse comes in.

"Excuse me, gentlemen. I just need to change the IV and clean a few wounds, and then you can get back to your visit." She draws the curtain around the bed for privacy.

"When can I get out of here?"

The guys start hooting and hollering.

I hear Aaron's voice through the curtains, "Come on pay up. I told you. Do I know her or do I know my her?"

"Nice going, kiddo. You've got the Irish luck on your side."

"Nice try old man. Cough it up!"

I shake my head and smile.

"You have a wonderful family," Nurse Page says as she cleans my wounds. "So, which one of those two hotties is the baby daddy?"

Suddenly it's completely silent on the other side of the curtain.

"You're actually making fantastic progress. The wounds are almost completely running clear, which means the damage inside has healed or at least healing." She pauses.

"Luckily you don't have any broken bones, considering you were hit by a car. Just a few fractures. Right now, we're just monitoring for head trauma and sudden internal ruptures, but my guess is you'll be out of here in a few days."

She finishes up but turns and waves a warning finger. "I'm telling you, even after you're released, you need to take it easy. Don't push your body." She pulls back the curtain.

"I'm done, gentlemen."

"So, the big fish?"

They look at me, defeated.

"Nothing, huh? Are the tech people done with the stuff in my pack? Can I have it back, please?

"Sure, we'll have someone bring it over. But for now, you rest. We'll stop by later tonight."

"OK. Bye, guys. Bye, kiddo."

Max replies with "Bye, cupcake," and Aaron hits him in the arm. "She's talking to me!"

They're barely out of the door before I drift off as if I've been awake for days. Someone in my room rouses me from my sleep. It's the nurse from earlier.

"Oh, hey. Sorry to wake you. I was about to go off duty and the police dropped this by for you. Wanted to make sure you had it before I go."

"Thank you so much, Nurse Page."

"Oh, honey, please call me Natalie."

She sees me trying to sit up. "Oh, you won't be able to do it by yourself for a while. Let me show you. This is the remote for that little TV up there. This is to call the nurse, and this is to raise and lower the bed. "

"Thank you."

"No problem. My pleasure." She follows my eyes and then puts her hand on her hip.

"You want the box so you can work, don't you?" She picks it up.

"Ok, here you go. Enjoy, I guess."

"Have a great evening."

"You too, hon."

I open the lid. Something about what my dad said about Irish Luck or Luck of the Irish reminded me of the Prince Edward ring on the finger in the box. The finger is gone, thank God, but the ring is there. I remember Olivia having a similar one in eleventh grade. I take the phone out and start it up so I can listen to voicemails.

It turns into a nightmare when I figure out how painful it is to hit delete on a hundred messages. It takes nearly two hours to get to Olivia's message and the ones before. Mom asking for money, my boss asking me to let them know if I'll be returning to work, two heavy breathers, and then the last one makes my blood run cold.

I hit save and then went through all the mail, all standard except for one from the Department of Corrections. The message and the call are about the release of John Matthew Hickey. I haven't thought of that man in years. He is good-looking and younger than my mom but an absolute letch.

Olivia, however, didn't mind. She loved the attention and used every excuse in the book to come over or be alone with him. That summer I went away to Boston as I did every year, but when I look back at it now, the change in her wasn't subtle it was grandiose. There's an officer posted in front of my door, but after several attempts to call him, I pick up the phone and call Adrian.

While I'm waiting for Adrian to answer, my mind twists and turns as I go through the rest of the mail. I find four more postcards. There's nothing special about them. Not like the fifth with my parents on it. The others are generic run-of-the-mill touristy postcards. The fifth one, the last one, is what I focus on for the next half hour before everyone arrives.

Now that I'm feeling better, I'm remembering more about the ordeal. I remember falling down the hill, and being dumped into a grave but not being buried alive. Why? I remember I was groggy, and there was something familiar about the...

Adrian answers, and I ask him to round everyone up and come to the hospital.

"Why didn't the officer posted at your door call?" I can hear the fear in his voice. It makes me anxious.

"He's not answering, I've called him like ten times."

He exhales hard. He's panicking and now so am I.

"Alex, I need you to listen to me very carefully. I need you to try and get up and go and lock yourself in the bathroom. Get out of there now."

It's excruciating trying to lift myself up, never mind getting out of bed. I feel like I'm taking forever, and my body isn't cooperating, which frustrates me even more. I move slowly and check if there's a lock on the door. There isn't.

I have to get to the bathroom like he said. I am moving as fast as I can while holding onto the IV stand, but I have to pull it out or I won't go anywhere. I hear movement behind me. I turn to see the officer returning with a cup of coffee.

Fucking hell. I was scared out of my mind. He turns to check on me and sees me just standing there bleeding from the needle I've just pulled out of my arm. He yells for the nurse, who comes into the room. I can't see her face, only long blond hair. I managed to catch a glimpse of her name tag. It says, *Natalie Page.*

Panic begins to rise in me again. I pull the officer towards me and whisper in his ear that the woman in the room is not Natalie Page, but he dismisses me. I try to get up and get away but the officer slumps over me. His weight traps me while my killer walks towards me.

Breaking Point

I struggle to move, but it's nearly impossible to get the officer off me. My left hand has so many fractures I can barely use it, and my right hand is all I have to push him off. I can only move him down to my knees and pray that I will be able to pull my legs out from under him.

Olivia stares at me the whole time. Doesn't move. Doesn't say a word. Her bright blue eyes are dead. There's nothing behind them. I manage to pull my right leg free, and while I try to free the left one, she plunges a scalpel into my thigh. I scream in agony.

"Why are you doing this? What's wrong with you?"

It was the wrong thing to say, and she loses it and plunges the scalpel even deeper, twisting it this time. I want to pass out from the pain, but I can't, I won't. I notice the officer's taser clipped to his belt. I use my right hand to throw a jug of water at her, and while she ducks, I unclip the pepper spray. She laughs at my botched attempt at hitting her with the jug.

"You missed." She sounds like a 16-year-old girl.

"Did I?" I lift my right hand and hit her with the pepper spray in the face.

She screams bloody murder and falls to her knees. I finally free my left leg from under the officer's torso. I fall to the floor, and my entire body feels the wave of pain that travels through it. I have to move and think quickly.

The effects of the pepper spray won't last long. I have to decide whether to try to climb over the officer or crawl between the bed and his legs. The latter is safer if I don't want to injure myself any further, I reason.

Olivia's washing her face at the basin. I crawl slowly underneath the officer in the space between the floor and his legs. His sidearm is still in its holster. I don't believe in guns, but I take it out anyway. It weighs a ton.

The pepper spray is still making it impossible for her to see, no matter how much water she uses. I can either try and make it to the bathroom and lock myself in or run out, but how far would I get, and how many more people would get hurt? Olivia is clearly deranged, but what does this have to do with me?

My mind flashes back to John Hickey.

"This is about that scumbag John, isn't it?"

It's all slowly making sense. The girls who disappeared and were never found. The two girls and I in high school had testified against him. We'd sent him to jail, and she blamed us. So, she's been picking the girls off one at a time. All this because we sent him to jail.

"It started that way, but then I figured out I could kill two birds with one stone. Prepare a paradise of young women that he could indulge himself in when he got out and make us rich while I did it. You won't believe what these pervs are willing to pay for a young girl. And yes, sometimes they go further, and we have to hide the evidence. But it was fun."

"You're fucking crazy."

"Crazy in love."

"When he got out of jail, I went to meet him. Told him what I'd done. I wanted him to be proud of me."

She dabs her eyes with tissue paper. They're bright red from the pepper spray, but she can see. Best not to make sudden moves. Keep her talking.

"Let me guess, he wasn't interested?"

"He called me washed up and crazy. Me! He made me what I am. The things I did to make him happy. Under your nose even under the nose of that drunkard of a mother of yours. Do you know he once fucked me while she lay passed out on the couch and you were upstairs studying as usual."

"He passed me around to friends, older men, and I did it just to make him happy, and then you and those other sluts go and ruin it by lying and sending him to jail. Then he gets out and I'm not good enough. Tells me I'm a sinner, an abomination, and must repent!"

"So, you cut his finger off and sent it to me with the postcards."

She stares at me for a moment.

"What postcards?"

I hear the elevator doors open down the corridor and I know it's Adrian and Max. I make a break for the door, but she's faster than me.

She smashes my head into the floor and whispers, "Where do you think you're going?"

She lifts me up just as the guys reach the door.

"Let her go, Olivia. It's over."

"It will never be over. Don't you get it? I'm just one of thousands. Besides, Alex and I have a death pact we made as kids. We'd get married together, have kids together, and eventually die together. Right, friend?"

"I know we didn't get to the other part, but what the hell. A pact is still a pact."

She starts pulling me towards the open window and whispers to me, "Remember how you always wanted to know what it feels like to fly?" As she starts leaning out of the window and pulling me with her, Adrian screams.

"Possum!"

I let my entire body go limp and drop to the floor. The gun falls from the front of my waistband, and she grabs it and points it at me. A shot rings out. When I open my eyes, she's gone. Like a bad dream.

Adrian helps me up and back into bed. He calls in the cavalry. This is one for the books for the forensic guys. I could have looked out of the window to see her broken body and be sure that she was really dead. I don't. Olivia Sinclair died a long time ago.

One thing keeps nagging at me, though. If she hadn't sent the postcards, who did, and why? I ask one of the officers to bring them to me while the others mill around waiting for something to do, or just out of curiosity. He takes them out of the box and hands them to me. I pull the tray table towards me and fan them out. They're like a puzzle that needs figuring out.

Max comes in, followed by Adrian, who's just set my mind at ease.

"What are you looking at Harper?"

"These postcards. I think that some of the missing girls are buried in the Riverview Cemetery, possibly under other coffins, but these postcards are some kind of map."

Adrian moves closer.

"A map of the dead. I think this is a clue to where the other girls are buried."

"Do you think you can figure it out?"

Max looks at it and can't make heads or tails of it.

"If anyone can, she can."

I stare intently at the cards and move them around as carefully as I would a prized puzzle piece. The shapes begin to form, and it hits me. They're not co-ordinates. They're star constellations but placed on Earth. The general outline is very familiar.

"It's the cemetery where paupers are buried. I recognize the edges. It's a unique shape. John Hickey sent me this."

"How can, you be sure?"

"It was the only thing we ever had in common."

"He knew I'd understand." I lie back and feel the full weight of exhaustion overtake me.

"What about the fifth one with your parents on it? It doesn't have any symbols or indication of a burial ground."

Max turns it over and over.

"Yes, it does. It's where she buried him. She was obsessed with that picture when we were kids. Wanted a love like that. He knew she was going to kill him and where she would bury him."

"He just wanted someone to find him and give him a proper burial and those girls too."

"Why, though? He was a bad man, but he wasn't a soulless one. He wanted to make things right. Like she said he found God in prison."

After the nurses and doctors came and attended to me. They poked and prodded for hours to make sure there was nothing life-threatening, especially the scalpel wound. And then I think they gave me a horse tranquilizer because I slept for three days.

Healing Wounds

Max sits on the edge of the hospital bed and just looks at me.

"What? Stop being so weird." He looks at me seriously, then takes my hand. "You've been the only constant in my life, do you know that?"

"No, I didn't. You're always so suave and sophisticated. I thought you had it all together."

"No one has it all together, Harper. We all have dragons and demons to slay. Some of our own making and others we inherit. But whatever hand life deals you, you play it."

"Okay, you're scaring me. What's going on?"

"I honestly don't know. These past few weeks with you and the things we've gone through together have just given me time to think. I need to leave Riverview. I'll either find my place out there or my way back here, but either way, I have to go."

"I get that. I understand, but is it selfish of me to want you to stay?"

"Kinda, yeah." We both laugh. Although it still hurts when I do, it's worth it.

"I'm going to miss you so badly. "

"I'm going to miss you and your smart-ass remarks." I blink away tears.

"I really am going to miss you." He gets up.

"So, when are you leaving? Right now? You're not going to stick around for the trials?"

"Stay and watch a bunch of rich pricks try and weasel their way out of statutory rape, assault, and murder charges? No thanks. It's going to be a circus."

"I know, and I'm already being touted as the Ringmaster." I exhale.

Maybe I'll use that time and take Aaron on a road trip. Homeschool him for a few months. All of this has brought up a lot of memories and truths for me. I have a Dad and a foster son now. I worry sometimes that I'm too broken to be of any good to either of them.

"My dad is dealing with sorting out his family's dirty laundry and scandals. It's not easy on him. I think he needs me and Aaron here. We keep him sane. He left this place to have a wholesome life with the woman he loved, and now he's back here in the thick of it all."

"You know when all that stuff was happening with Olivia, I actually felt sorry for her?"

"Really?"

"Yes. She just wanted to be loved. And she found it with someone who didn't find it with her. Does that make sense? How many of us go through our whole lives and never really live or love."

He looks at me for a while.

"You may be onto something there, Harper."

He turns to leave but comes back. He kisses me slowly and sensually, and even with the pain I'm in, my body comes alive. Then he's gone. I lie there for hours afterward, nurses coming in and out, changing tubes, administering medication, and I just stare off into the distance.

Isn't it weird the turns life takes? I had to leave Riverview and come back to find out who I was and to reckon with my past. One of us fell in love and idolized the monster while the rest of us burnt him at the stake.

All these years later in death, he's helping bring closure to dozens of families. Families whose daughters left one night and never came back. As awful as he was when we knew him and sent him to prison, something happened in there that changed him enough to take responsibility for the monster he helped create and to try and make it right, even though he knew it would cost him his life. He gave it happily.

I have a father now and new family members to get to know. A foster son I need to raise into the kind of man the world needs. As I lie here, I have no clue as to how I'm going to do it. Max is leaving to find his place in the world, who he is outside of the criminal-slash-bad boy he's condemned to be here. He's daring to find a new destiny for himself, no matter what that turns out to be.

I'm not sure I have that kind of bravery in me. I have a father and kid I love: is that enough to call a life? The cold hard truth is I don't know who Alex Harper is now. Not what she has done or can do but at her core, who is she, and do I have the courage to stay in Riverview and find out or do I run and reinvent myself into someone else? It's easier than people think.

News vans are camped outside the hospital 24/7. Every visitor has to be screened to make sure that they're not journalists or bloggers hoping for an exclusive. I've been moved four times now. It's been a week since Olivia died and that chapter closed for all of us, but it's taken a horrific toll on all of us emotionally, mentally, and physically.

Adrian has been hit the hardest by this. He was honored and celebrated for a few days after but then given desk duty because his celebrity was a hindrance to the effective execution of his duties. As he explained to me, in political speak it means that he got the wrong people in trouble, and he was going to pay for it one way or another.

I didn't know if there was a way out for him or even a way back. Once you were branded a liability in law enforcement, especially for pissing off important people and airing their dirty laundry, you were dead in the water, career-wise. People don't realize how much politics plays into other branches of civil service, especially law enforcement.

Now a good man, an excellent detective, is confined to desk duty until they frustrate him enough to leave. That's the plan, he says. They have no grounds to dismiss him, and even if they did, the public outcry would torpedo the upcoming gubernatorial elections.

I just have to figure my own shit out and be there for him when he needs it. He's my friend, and he saved my life. Even though I'm unsure of a lot of things, the one thing I do know is I have people who love and care for me and will show up for me when I need them and vice versa. All in all, it's not such a bad starting place for a new life in progress.

Bonus 1st Chapter - Shrouded Shame

The next installment in the Alex Harper series:

The last thing I remember is walking into the police station to have coffee with my friend Detective Adrian Miller. Adrian had been 'benched' for three months after uncovering a trafficking ring that sent dozens of the town's rich and famous to prison, and some were still on trial or being investigated.

"I remember walking towards Adrian and then nothing. I woke up and he was carrying me out of the building."

"And then what happened?"

"I gained consciousness for a few minutes and then passed out again." The agents interrogating me were from the FBI and they'd swooped down on Riverview like Fish Eagles when a bomb was detonated inside the police station. "When can I see Adrian... Detective Miller?"

"You won't be able to for a while, he's been placed in an induced coma until doctors feel his body is healed enough to maintain its normal function."

I break down immediately, but neither one of them even bothers to offer me Kleenex.

"Which room is he in? Which floor?"

"Let me make this clear to you, Ms. Harper: you are not to go anywhere near Detective Miller. Is that understood?"

"Look, I get the jarhead hairstyle fresh from war, my way or the highway military attitude, but here's where you listen to me. I may have just been blown across the room at a police station, but if you think that you're going to march in here and get in my face and bully me into submission, you've got the shock of your life coming! No one tells me what I can and can't do! I survived being shot at, stabbed, being buried alive! I brought down one of the biggest human trafficking rings in the Pacific Northwest. You don't scare me."

"Listen, little girl..."

I looked at his partner, clearly a rookie and probably subjected to this every day, but I just got blown up I had no time-pause button for this.

"Little girl?" I grab him so hard in the nuts that his scream shatters a glass vase. "Who's the little girl now?"

I take my clothes and go to the empty room next door to change. I slip into jeans and a T-shirt and am about to leave when a large hand covers my mouth, and someone whispers, "Shh... don't scream." I know the voice. I turn around and it's him, Max.

"What are you doing here?"

"Well, I was in Iowa and saw on the news that someone had tried to kill you two again and figured you might need my help."

"I thought you were off finding yourself?"

"Hey, I can multitask."

"No, you can't. I've seen you try."

"So, spill it."

"I can't. I don't even know what's going on. One minute I'm walking into the police station to meet Adrian for coffee, and the next thing I wake up here. The worst part is I'm getting the impression that they're trying to pin it on him."

"What?"

"Yeah. Some kind of hero complex. Got a taste for the fame and now wants to hog the spotlight again."

"What do you think is going on?

"Honestly, I think it's an excuse to get him out and weaken the cases against the governor's besties who face 140 years in prison because of all the shit they've caught on that came out during the investigation. They don't care about the bombing. It was probably a gas main of something, but when those reports get issued, I can promise you that's not what they're going to say."

"Just like ole times, huh?"

"No, Max. This is next-level shit. When you get in the government's crosshairs, you know you're fucked. Our whole lives are on computers, phones, microchips, our calls get monitored, and they even know which flavor coffee you like."

Max looks at me as though I'm paranoid. I lift my hand.

"It's cool. I'm going to get home to my dad and kid and convince them to go off-grid. I just need to know that they're safe before I fling myself into the lions' den wearing a meat dress."

"Okay, I'm going to call around and see how much information I can dig up about what's going on."

"Just make sure you use burner phones. Unless there's something that you actually do want them to know."

"Alex. Come on, this is a little out there even for you."

"I can see why you'd think that way, so let's do this. Call a friend of yours and tell him you're passing through town on your way to Seattle. And to meet you for coffee."

"Seriously!?"

I just stare at him and say nothing. I'm done arguing my case.

He makes the call, and ten minutes later, his friend arrives. Five minutes after that, he's being dragged out of the coffee shop and interrogated.

I just raise my eyebrows because there's nothing more to say. This is bigger than all three of us.

"You know Olivia warned us? Remember before she died, she said there were thousands like her, and we didn't win that day. "

"What kind of world are we living in, Max, if the people who do the right thing get villainized while the wrongdoers, the monsters, and despots get rewarded or protected?"

"I know you guys don't always see eye to eye, but he's a good man. He did the right thing. How does he end up a person of interest and under lockdown while he's in a medically induced coma?"

"Shit! That's hectic. My dad had to be placed in one. Pretty serious."

I get up and go to the window on the door.

"OK, the coast is clear. We need to get out of here first and then lie low while we figure everything out.!"

I leave first, and then Max. We walk out of the building and onto the street. There's no time to celebrate. We need to find a place to hide out until we know what's going on. Luckily neither of us is a person of interest in the bombing, but that doesn't mean that there isn't a BOLO out for us.

Policemen all over the city have probably been given our pics and stats and a hold-for-questioning order. Max knows the drill, for god's sake. I learned most of it from him when we were kids.

We walk slowly but purposefully until we come to one of those motels that don't ask too many questions and aren't very cooperative with law enforcement. The man at the reception desk barely looks at us. Nothing to see, nothing to report. We get to the room, which is spare but looks maintained well enough. It's not going to get a Michelin star or whatever the hell they give hotels, but it's habitable. Now the test: I turn on the shower, and yay, it works... and after a few minutes, yay, hot water.

Max comes in carrying s packet of meds. "Are you sick?"

"No, but you were blown up. I'm fine."

"I'll be the judge of that."

"Used that line a lot, huh? Drives the girls wild, I'll bet. OW!"

"Sorry. Okay, you have a lot of cuts and scrapes, so you might want to bite down hard on one of those pillows."

"Hard pass. I have no idea where that pillow's been."

"Ok so just bite down on your T-shirt or brave it!"

"OW! God dammit!"

"Sorry, I thought you were ready."

"Wait a minute. Did you say I have a lot of cuts and scrapes on my back?"

"Yeah, so what? "

"If the force of the bomb came from the front, then my face and torso would have the damage. I was blown forward, not backward."

Small Town Shadows:

Decrypting the Clues in Watson Bay

Thank you for reading Shrouded Deception, feel free to leave a an honest review if you'd like. If you enjoyed the mystery of Hacker Alex Harper, dive into the Novella Small town Shadows – Parker Rose Mystery.

Small Town Shadows

In the art-stained shadows of Watson Bay, a new gallery sparks more than just controversy. When Jack, an outsider, discovers a body at his Art Gallery, they call on Parker Rose, the town's part-time hacker, to investigate the case. Parker's hacking skills unearth a sinister past, linking Jack to a vanished ex-girlfriend. The bartender goes missing in the town, adding to the mystery. Their paths cross in danger and desire. Accusations are thrown around and Parker discovers another dead body and now she's being chased by Jack and a mysterious person in a hood. Parker's world is at risk as trust becomes unstable and a shocking revelation emerges. In a pulse-pounding revelation, Parker and Jack unravel a web of deception, exposing a small-town sheriff with sinister motives. The quiet town conceals not only a murderer but a mastermind pulling the strings. Can Parker and Jack become heroes, or will the secrets of Watson Bay stay hidden? The truth awaits—a dance between darkness and desire.

Small Town Shadows:

Chapter 1:

Parker Rose paled as she looked at the body. With her arms folded across her chest and her beige rain jacket pulled tightly around her like a blanket, she failed to move beyond the foyer. She hadn't seen anything like this before; not in her quiet abode of Watson Bay. Ever since she had gotten into Private Investigation, she mostly dealt with security breaches and expenditure reports for small businesses. She tracked expenses for the financially inept and found malicious hardware installed by computer viruses derived from some unsavory internet browsing. But never had she encountered a dead body.

Standing in the middle of the art gallery, Parker felt exposed. The wall behind her was made entirely of glass, which usually enabled passersby to marvel at the peculiar art adorning the walls, but now it felt like a threat. She was exposed, her back turned to the evils that were lurking in her supposedly safe town. Even the presence of the police didn't do much to quell her nerves.

Sheriff Heston strode over to her, his hands snugly in the waistband of his slacks. He shook his head as he evaluated the blood that had pooled out of the victim, painting the wood floors a stomach-churning crimson.

"No sign of forced entry," he announced, taking his hat off his head and wiping his brow, "we don't know who this young man is, either."

"An outsider?" Parker squeaked. She was unable to break her gaze from the gruesome scene.

"Homeless, maybe. Can't tell how clean he is behind the—"

"Yeah," she cut him off. She didn't want to hear it. "Why'd you call me here, Sheriff?"

"You're the brightest girl this town's got."

"I don't investigate *murder*, though." Now, she was able to look at him. Her big eyes were brewing tears she would be embarrassed to be caught spilling. Despite the shock, she didn't want to garner a reputation for weakness. After all, getting into deadlier crime was a financial opportunity.

Download Small Town Shadows now to keep reading...

Don't miss out!

Visit the website below and you can sign up to receive emails whenever Stella Mace publishes a new book. There's no charge and no obligation.

https://books2read.com/r/B-A-KHASB-MWNPD

BOOKS 2 READ

Connecting independent readers to independent writers.

www.ingramcontent.com/pod-product-compliance
Lightning Source LLC
Chambersburg PA
CBHW071336150726
47997CB00002B/746